THE BOBBSEY TWINS AND
THE FLYING CLOWN

A MYSTERIOUS long-distance call for help from a boy named Howie marks the beginning of this spooky new adventure. It takes the Bobbsey Twins to the World of Fun in Florida and drops them smack in the middle of a baffling detective case. Howie's warning is no joke. The twins discover that he and his sister, an airplane pilot called the Flying Clown, are in serious danger, but why? Mixing fun with their sleuthing, Bert, Nan, Freddie and Flossie unravel a ball of knots to help nab an unusual gang of bad men.

Bert splashed into the swiftly running water!

The
Bobbsey Twins
and the
Flying
Clown

By

LAURA LEE HOPE

GROSSET & DUNLAP
Publishers • New York

PRINTED IN THE UNITED STATES OF AMERICA
LIBRARY OF CONGRESS CATALOG CARD NO. 73–16661
ISBN: 0–448–8067–6
The Bobbsey Twins and the Flying Clown

CONTENTS

CHAPTER I

RED-NOSE FREDDIE

"COME on, now, Flossie, climb higher!" said Bert. "Put one foot on Nan's shoulder and the other on mine!"

It was a rainy Sunday afternoon and the Bobbsey twins were playing circus in their basement. Bert and Nan, twelve, were standing on a mat, and Flossie, a wriggly six-year-old, was teetering on the top of the pyramid.

Just then the telephone rang upstairs and Mrs. Bobbsey called down. "Children, do you know anybody named Howie? He's calling collect from Florida."

"Who?" Bert asked as Flossie jumped down.

"Howie. He wants to talk to the Bobbsey twins. Says it's urgent."

The twins raced up to the living room. Their mother was undecided about accepting the call.

"If it's urgent," Nan said, "I think we'd better take it, Mother." She went to the telephone and put it to her ear. "Hello, Howie. This is Nan Bobbsey."

The voice on the other end sounded young and excited. "You're coming to the World of Fun, aren't you?"

"Yes. How did you know?"

"Never mind," the boy replied. "Look, there's a lot of trouble down here, so watch out."

"What do you mean?"

"I can't tell you now. I've got to go! They're chasing me! Good-by!"

The phone clicked and Nan looked at the others, amazement written on her face.

"Who's Howie? Bert asked.

"He didn't say."

"And how did he know we were going to Florida?" Freddie piped up.

"He didn't tell me that, either."

Mr. Bobbsey, who had been reading the Sunday paper, laid it aside. "Maybe it's some kind of a joke," he said.

"Howie didn't sound very funny," Nan said.

"Somebody's after him, and there's trouble in Florida."

"This certainly is strange," Bert declared.

The family had told a few close friends about their vacation trip to the World of Fun. But, as far as they knew, no one in Florida except the motel people had been informed of their plans.

"Maybe we're running into another mystery," Mrs. Bobbsey said with a laugh. "It wouldn't be the first time."

The Bobbseys were good detectives, and nearly everyone in their town of Lakeport knew about the cases they had solved.

"I think you'll have enough to do with all the amusements there," Mr. Bobbsey said with a chuckle. "And I doubt if we'll ever hear from this Howie what's-his-name again."

Freddie, meanwhile, had slipped off quietly, and when Bert, Nan and Flossie returned to the playroom, he was not there. Nan called upstairs.

"Freddie, where are you? It's your turn on top of the pyramid."

Still, Freddie did not appear, and Flossie said, "Oh, dear! What's that silly boy doing?"

Just as she started up the steps, Freddie came clomping down.

"Eeek!" Flossie cried.

Freddie's face was made up like a clown's. He

had big yellow lips, daubs of blue paint on his cheeks, and a red, red nose.

"You've been into my theater makeup kit!" Nan scolded. "I told you never to do that!"

"But it's my turn to be the top clown!" Freddie protested. "If I'm going to be one, I've got to look like one!"

"All right," Bert said. "Let's see if you can balance any better than Flossie."

The younger boy grinned with delight as he climbed on the shoulders of Bert and Nan. He swayed back and forth a few times, and then, with a "Whoop!" jumped down.

The force sent the older twins reeling backward, and both of them sat down hard on the mat.

"You're not supposed to jump off like that, Freddie!" said Bert.

The children practiced several more times, all the while talking about the mysterious telephone call from Howie.

When it was time for supper, the children went upstairs and their parents laughed at Freddie's makeup.

"I hope you put a foundation under that, young man," his mother said.

"What's a foundation?"

"Didn't you put grease on your face first?"

"No."

Freddie swayed back and forth.

"Then you'll never get that paint off!" his mother worried. "Come with me!" Mrs. Bobbsey took him into the bathroom and began to scrub off the colors, which made rainbow streaks on Freddie's face.

"We're doing pretty well," Mrs. Bobbsey said. "It looks fine except on your nose. That's still red."

At the supper table the children giggled about Freddie's red nose.

"And to think we're starting off to Florida tomorrow!" Mr. Bobbsey said with a sigh.

"Freddie looks like Rudolph, the red-nosed reindeer," Flossie said.

"But I can fly through the air better than you!" Freddie said.

Early the next morning the Bobbseys arrived at the local airport and not long afterward they were flying in a big airplane to Florida.

Freddie felt embarrassed about his nose and tried to hold a hand over his face. When he forgot to do this, other passengers stared at him.

"My goodness," one woman said, "you've got a sunburn already and we're not even in Florida!"

Finally the pilot announced that they were approaching the World of Fun. "You'll see it from the left side of the plane," he said.

The Bobbseys pressed close to the window to get a glimpse of their vacation spot.

"Look, there it is!" Bert said excitedly.

The World of Fun looked like a town, with parks and a waterway. It had colorful buildings along broad streets, a monorail with pretty cars, a large lagoon, and in the center a big volcano spitting out red fire.

"Oh, boy, this is keen!" Freddie said.

"And look at all the people!" Flossie exclaimed. "Oh, I hope we land soon!"

As the plane dropped lower and lower, Nan suddenly gasped and cried out, "I see a real flying clown!"

"Where?" Bert asked.

"Over there!"

"It's an airplane," Freddie declared.

"Sure, but look how it's painted," Nan replied.

The wings were outstretched arms, and the nose resembled a clown's head. The body was covered with stripes and polka dots.

"It's a pontoon plane," Mr. Bobbsey stated. "And it's going to land on that lagoon."

The children watched the craft touch down lightly, and before long their own big airliner landed at the jetport not far from the World of Fun.

After they had debarked and picked up their baggage, the Bobbsey family was paged by a man who said, "This way to the bus for the African Village."

Freddie wrinkled his red nose. "African Village? What's that, Daddy?"

"That's the name of the motel. We're going to live in huts. Didn't Mother tell you?"

"Huts? Oh, goody!" Flossie said.

"I don't know about that," Freddie replied. "Will there be wild animals walking around?"

"Of course not," Nan said.

They boarded a minibus which took them right into the World of Fun.

The children were amazed at the size of the place. "We could stay here a year," Nan said as they passed a gingerbread castle, "and still not go on all the rides!"

"Look how high that Ferris wheel is," Bert said.

Just then the clown airplane zipped overhead again. It flew so low that the Bobbseys could see the lettering on the underside.

"The Flying Clown!" Nan read. "That's its real name!"

The bus drove into a compound filled with thatched huts arranged about a large swimming pool.

"Well, here we are," Mr. Bobbsey said as his family piled out. He went to the office and signed the guest register while the children raced to the poolside.

"Boy, are we going to have fun!" Bert said

and bent over to dabble his hands in the water.

In a few minutes Mr. and Mrs. Bobbsey came to the pool with a pleasant-looking young woman. Nan gasped when she saw her. "Mrs. Mingo!" she said. "What are you doing here?"

Mary Mingo had been Bert and Nan's second-grade teacher. She had left Lakeport when her husband was transferred to Florida.

"Hello, children," she said, putting an arm around the twins. "Goodness, how big you've grown since you were in my class!"

Mrs. Mingo told them she was the motel manager and had been delighted when she had received the Bobbseys' reservation.

"I have a message for you," she said. "It has your name on it, but it's spelled wrong."

Nan took the letter. On it in black printing were the words, "For the Bobsie Twins."

The girl opened it. Inside was a note. It said: "Mete me here tonite. Howie."

CHAPTER II

THE GIANT SHAKE

"OH, how nice!" Mrs. Mingo said. "Is Howie a friend of yours?"

"We never met him," Nan replied. "But he called us and asked if we were coming to the World of Fun. He mentioned that there was a lot of trouble down here."

"Do you know what he meant?" Bert asked his former teacher.

"Well," Mrs. Mingo hesitated, "there has been some trouble, but we tried to keep it out of the newspapers."

"Can you tell us about it?"

"I'd rather not, because I haven't got all the facts. Talk to Mr. Peter Prescott. He's in charge of security for the World of Fun. Tell him I told you to contact him, and explain about Howie."

"We'll call him right now," Mr. Bobbsey said.

"Good. I'll have to get back to the office. Come visit me any time."

The Bobbseys went to the three huts assigned to them and began hanging up their clothes.

Bert was finished first and telephoned Mr. Prescott, whose office was located in the Gingerbread Castle. He was very cordial and invited the family to meet with him next day.

"Is everybody settled in?" Mrs. Bobbsey called out as she walked past the boys' hut.

"We are!" Freddie said. He and Bert dashed outside. The girls were ready, too, and all were eager to get on with their Florida adventure.

"Let's ride the monorail first," Mr. Bobbsey suggested.

Flossie jumped up and down, clapped her hands, and raced on ahead. It was only a short walk to the station, where they climbed the steps and waited a few minutes until the next train pulled in.

The younger twins skipped aboard, followed by Bert, Nan, and their parents. With wide eyes, the visitors gazed over the vast expanse of buildings, rides, and exhibits. There was also a canal. It started and ended at the lagoon, and circled around a large building on which there was a sign saying, "Niagara Falls and Rapids."

"I want to go there! Let's go there!" Freddie cried out.

"Yes, let's," Flossie chimed in. "I'd love to ride the rapids."

"Later," Nan said. "I'm getting hungry."

"Me, too," her father said with a grin. "What say we go for a snack?"

"Oh, Daddy, you are bee-yoo-ti-ful!" Flossie exclaimed.

Nan spied a large sign which read, "Giant Shakes, 25¢."

"That's what I want," she declared. "A giant milk shake would taste good right now."

Mrs. Bobbsey looked a little dubious as they approached the building. It had a ticket booth in front and a small entrance door. "This doesn't look like a refreshment place to me," she said.

"Oh, come on, Mother!" Freddie said. "It said so!"

Bert paid the money for the tickets and the family entered. Inside it was very dim. They could see no tables or chairs, only ghostly looking signs on the walls. The floor was softly padded.

Suddenly the room began to shake. Flossie

screamed and clutched Nan's hand. All the Bobbseys hung on to one another in order to keep their balance. But the floor kept shaking, and all at once the whole family went down. *Plop!*

The shaking stopped as suddenly as it had started. Overhead lights went on brightly and everyone laughed. All over the room people were getting up. Two little girls had begun to cry, but burst into giggles when they saw that others, too, had been fooled by the Giant Shakes.

The Bobbseys filed out into the sunshine and looked for a real refreshment place. Just as they noticed a hamburger stand, Nan said, "Where's Freddie?"

Everyone turned around, but Freddie was not in sight. "Maybe he's still in the Giant Shakes," Flossie spoke up.

"Run back and see, will you, Bert?" Mr. Bobbsey said. "We'll meet you at the hamburger place over there."

"Okay." Bert went to the ticket booth and explained to the man that his little brother might still be inside.

"Go ahead, take a look," the man said.

Bert went in, and as his eyes became accustomed to the dim light, he saw Freddie talking to another boy.

All at once the family went down.

"Are you going to be surprised!" he was saying.

"Come on, Freddie," Bert called out.

"I want to stay and have some more shakes," Freddie replied with a big wink at his brother.

"Not now," Bert said. He put an arm around Freddie's shoulder and hustled him outside. They caught up with the others at the refreshment stand and ordered milk shakes and hamburgers.

While they were sitting at the counter, three bears skipped past, bowing and cavorting like young cubs. Following them were two cowboys. They wore wide-brimmed hats and blue jeans and carried lariats.

All at once, one of them uncoiled his rope and swung a big loop. He tossed it over the Baby Bear and pulled the animal clown toward him.

"Oh, dear!" Flossie said. "What is he going to do with the poor little bear?"

Just then the Mother and Father Bear grabbed the cowboy and took the lasso from around their baby's head.

Nan got up and hurried over to the Mother Bear. "Is anything wrong?" she asked. "Are the cowboys being mean to you?"

A girl's voice replied, "Oh, no. The cowboys are really policemen. They have fun with us all the time."

One of the cowboys had overheard Nan's question. "We're just clowning around with the clowns," he said, laughing.

After lunch, the children went on various rides, and in the afternoon had ice cream and soda. Finally, the tired family returned to their motel. They had a refreshing swim in the pool, then went to supper. Later, they stretched out on lounge chairs by the poolside to watch the sunset.

Freddie and Flossie could not sit quietly too long. They spied a sandbox and walked off to join several other children their own age. The older twins remained with their parents and discussed the mystery of Howie.

"What time do you think he'll show up?" Mrs. Bobbsey asked.

Bert shrugged. "I hope not too late, or else we'll all be in bed!"

Mrs. Bobbsey was just as curious as her children. "I wonder how old he is," she said. "You heard his voice, Nan. What would you say?"

"Between eight and twelve," Nan said. "My guess is that he has blond hair and is sort of skinny."

Bert chuckled. "I think he's dark-haired and fat."

The soft breeze cooled off the hot day as it grew darker. Finally, Mrs. Bobbsey stood up.

"Nan," she said, "help me put the young ones to bed."

They all left except Bert, who remained in case Howie appeared. A few yellow lights shone on the palm trees and palmetto bushes surrounding the pool. Bert was nearly lulled to sleep. Then, through drooping eyelids, he noticed someone walking on the other side of the pool.

It looked like a bearded, gray-haired man with a cane. He had a large nose and clear bright eyes. As he came close to Bert, he whispered, "Are you a Bobbsey boy?"

"Yes, I'm Bert."

"I'm Howie. If you're a detective, as I've heard, you can help me!"

Just then, Nan came out. When Howie saw her, he started to run.

"Wait, come back!" Bert called. "That's my sister Nan!"

She, too, was amazed to see the boy in the funny disguise. After Bert had introduced her, Nan said, "What's the trouble, Howie? And why are you in disguise?"

The boy drew closer and said in a very low voice, "It's about the Flying Clown. She's my——"

There was a noise in the bushes behind them. All three turned to see a tall man jump out.

His face looked like a mask, with glowing eyes and an open mouth showing large, sharp teeth. He made such a horrible, growling noise that all three children froze in terror.

"Help!" Nan tried to cry out, but her voice was only a whisper. The man sprang toward Howie, and the boy took off like a flash, dashing to the other side of the pool.

Nan was unable to move and Bert took her hand. But the intruder did not bother the Bobbseys. Instead, he raced after Howie.

"Come back here, you!" he demanded. His voice sounded sharp and he raised an arm menacingly.

Howie kept running and so did the man. His long legs gained quickly on the boy who raced around the pool for the second time.

"Come on," Bert whispered to Nan. "We've got to help Howie!"

But before the twins could make a move, the boy turned quickly and threw his cane. The man tripped over it and with a gurgling cry fell headlong into the water!

CHAPTER III

A GANG OF THIEVES

WHILE Howie ran away, the man splashed and floundered about in the deep water.

"Help! Help!" he called out. "I can't swim!"

Bert and Nan dived in, surfaced on either side of him and towed him to the shallow end of the pool. The man coughed and spluttered as he staggered out.

The twins saw that his face was now very different. In fact, they had never seen a face like it before. A long chin and high forehead gave the impression of a football. The nose was thin and pinched, and the ears stood out like question marks.

But the most noticeable thing was a broad

scar that ran from the side of his mouth to his left earlobe.

The man's small eyes glittered defiantly. "Wait till I get my hands on that kid!" he fumed between coughs. "And you two stay out of this, understand!"

The twins were amazed, but before they could ask any questions, the man raced through the palmettos.

Bert and Nan followed for a while, until they saw him climb over a fence behind the African Village and disappear. They returned to the pool to find their parents looking for them.

"My goodness!" Mrs. Bobbsey said. "Why did you go swimming in your clothes?"

"It was an emergency," Bert explained and told what had happened.

"And he didn't even say 'thank you' for rescuing him!" Nan declared.

"He was wearing a mask," Bert said. "It's probably at the bottom of the pool. And look, here's the cane. It's the souvenir kind."

It was agreed they would look for the mask early next morning. Bert rose at sunrise. He woke up Nan while the younger twins still slept soundly and they skinned into their bathing suits.

Heavy dew covered the vegetation outside and birds were singing. The air smelled sweet.

Bert and Nan went to the pool and looked down into the deep water.

"I see something!" Bert said.

"Me, too. I'll bet that's the mask!"

Bert dived in with Nan streaking down through the water beside him. He grasped the object and they moved to the surface.

"That's it, all right," Bert said, climbing out.

"Ugh, what a horrible expression!" Nan commented.

"Try it on!" Bert suggested.

Nan slipped the mask over her face. Just then Flossie came out of her hut. She looked at Nan and gasped. Then she dashed back inside.

"You'd better take that thing off before you scare her to pieces," Bert said.

Flossie peeked out again, saw the older twins laughing, and ran over to examine the clue.

"Go get Freddie," Nan said. "We want to search around this place. Maybe we'll find something else."

Sleepy-eyed Freddie arrived a few minutes later with his sister. Together the four began a careful search of the bushes and the area between the pool and the back fence. Freddie was like a hound dog, head bent low, moving back and forth to examine every inch of ground.

Finally he called out, "Hey, Bert, what's this thing?"

Flossie looked at Nan and gasped.

His brother came over and picked up a soft blob of something. They examined it.

"That's putty," said Nan. "The same kind I have in my theatrical kit."

Bert snapped his fingers. "I know. Howie was wearing a false nose. It fell off while he was getting away!"

"If we only knew what he really looks like," Nan said, "it would be easier to find him."

At breakfast the children recounted their new adventure. Their father asked, "Do you think you could identify that man if you saw him again?"

"Oh, sure," Bert said.

"And we know he can't swim," Nan added. "That might be a good clue."

"Like Hank, the cowboy we once met," Bert said.

"Speaking of cowboys," Mrs. Bobbsey said, "let's go see Mr. Prescott and try to get to the bottom of this mystery about Howie."

They walked a short distance to a street on which there was a horse-drawn trolley car.

"All aboard!" the conductor called out. "Last stop, the Gingerbread Castle!"

The horse clomped through the crowds of smiling people. Just before they arrived at their destination, they passed the Rainbow Novelty Shop, its front decorated in a riot of colors. A sign in the window announced, "Swiss Day Sale." Various cuckoo clocks and watches were on display.

"I'd love to have a beautiful Swiss watch," Nan said.

About two hundred yards farther on, the trolley stopped and the Bobbseys got off in front of the Gingerbread Castle. A small sign beside the entrance read: Administration.

The children ran ahead through the door and up to a woman who sat behind the information desk.

"We have an appointment with Mr. Prescott," Nan said. "We're the Bobbseys."

The woman smiled. "Wait here until I call his office." She spoke briefly on the telephone. A few seconds later a tall cowboy approached them.

"Come with me. Mr. Prescott is waiting," he said, and ushered them through several offices in which there were lots of cowboys seated at desks, answering telephones or studying huge wall maps of the World of Fun.

Finally the family was led into a small room, where a handsome young man greeted them. He put out his hand to Mr. Bobbsey. "I'm Peter Prescott. Just call me Pete, all of you."

Introductions were made. Then the Bobbseys took seats next to Mr. Prescott's large desk.

He sat on the edge of it, with one leg swinging, and said, "I hear you have some information for me."

"Plenty of it," Nan said. "We hardly know where to begin."

"First tell me about Howie," the security chief said. "He seems to be the big mystery around here."

The Bobbseys reported all they knew about the boy, including the chase the night before, when his pursuer had fallen into the pool. Before they could show Pete the clues they had found, he shook his head.

"I feel sorry for this boy," he said. "Howie's name is Norton. He lives with his sister Cherry in a house trailer not far from the World of Fun.

"That is, he used to live there before he ran away. Now it seems he's spending all his time at the World of Fun, eating hot dogs and sleeping wherever he can find a sheltered place."

Pete sighed and went on, "Several people have seen him, but whenever someone tries to speak to him, he runs away."

Prescott opened his desk and removed a picture. "This is Howie Norton."

The Bobbseys passed it around. Howie was a nice-looking boy, slender, with blond hair, dancing eyes and a straight, slender nose covered with freckles.

"Howie mentioned something about a flying clown," Nan spoke up.

"Well, you see," Pete explained, "his sister Cherry is an airplane pilot who flies our pontoon plane called *The Flying Clown.*"

The man said that Cherry Norton had had a sad experience. "She wanted to be an aerial clown and had attended the Jumbo Circus Clown School. But there was some kind of mixup and she left. It was quite unpleasant for her. And now she's even having trouble here at the World of Fun."

"What kind of trouble?" Freddie asked.

"Once the motor of her plane went dead, and she had to land on a river. The mechanic claimed it had been tampered with. Another time rumors were spread that she was a poor flyer and business fell off."

"Who are her enemies?" Nan asked.

"Who knows?" Pete shrugged. "But I have a feeling that Howie's disappearance is somehow tied up with his sister's troubles."

"Oh, by the way," Nan said, "here are some clues we found last night, Pete. I thought you'd like to see them."

She showed him the horror mask they had picked up from the bottom of the pool, and also the cane and putty nose that Howie had dropped.

The security chief examined the mask carefully. "This was taken from our costume department!"

"Where's that?" Bert asked.

"In the underground." Pete explained that there was a vast system of underground passages of storerooms beneath the World of Fun.

"Then the man who fell in the pool," Mrs. Bobbsey reasoned, "may have stolen the mask."

"Howie told us there was trouble around here," Bert spoke up. "What did he mean by that?"

"I'll let you in on it if you promise not to tell the whole World of Fun," Pete said.

"We promise!" Freddie said, and his parents smiled.

"We are being bothered by a ring of thieves. They are so slippery that we haven't been able to catch even one of them!"

"What do they steal?"

"Trinkets, big cartons of candy, fireworks, and all kinds of expensive souvenirs. And we can't figure out how they escape from the park with all the merchandise."

Pete was interrupted by the intercom on his desk. A man's voice said, "London Bridge is falling down! Repeat. London Bridge is falling down!"

CHAPTER IV

HORSEY RAINES

FROM the expression on Pete's face, the Bobbseys realized that something was wrong.

He spoke into the intercom. "Where did it happen?"

"The Rainbow Novelty Shop," came the answer.

"What's this all about?" Bert asked the security chief as he hastened to the door.

" 'London Bridge is falling down' is a code word for robbery. Come on. It's up the street!"

Pete and the Bobbseys dashed out. They were joined by two cowboys and all raced to the novelty shop.

Pete went in and spoke to the proprietor. He

was very agitated. "Swiss watches!" He fumed. "Very good ones! They vanished as if by magic!"

"Didn't you notice anyone around?" the security chief asked.

"A few of the animal clowns and some people browsing. That's all. In fact, business has been very quiet this morning."

The cowboys as well as the Bobbseys began asking passersby what animal clowns they had seen near the shop. A girl about Flossie's age said that Goldilocks had walked out of the store carrying her big basket.

When Nan reported this to Pete, he had his men round up all people wearing that costume who were in the area. Then he made a call to the costume department.

Ten minutes later two cowboys arrived at the shop with five Goldilocks. Three were high school age girls, two were boys. When questioned, they all said they had not been near the novelty shop!

"That was a false clue," Pete said. "The little girl must have been wrong."

"Maybe somebody stole one of the Goldilocks uniforms," Nan said.

"I've already checked that department," Pete said. "No Goldilocks suits are missing."

Bert asked, "Do you think the thief might be hiding out in your underground?"

"That's a possibility. How would you like to take a tour underneath the World of Fun?"

"That would be great!" Freddie clapped his hands. "When can we see your underworld?"

"The underground, not the underworld," Flossie said and giggled.

The security man thought for a moment. "How about tomorrow afternoon?"

"That would be fine," Mrs. Bobbsey agreed.

"I have an idea," Nan spoke up. "We could see Cherry in the morning and talk to her about Howie."

"She'll be able to tell you a lot more than I know," Pete said.

On the way back to their motel, the Bobbseys looked at the map of World of Fun. The seaplane dock was at the edge of the lagoon. To get there they would have to pass through a little street called Loony Lane.

"I wonder what's so loony about it," said Bert.

"I understand it has a lot of surprises," his mother replied. "You'll find out tomorrow."

Next morning Mr. and Mrs. Bobbsey went off to play golf, leaving Bert and Nan in charge of the younger twins.

"You know your way around," Mrs. Bobbsey

said. "Just be careful, and if you see that awful man, call one of the cowboys at once."

"Don't worry about us," Nan said. "And see if you can beat Daddy at golf again, Mother!" She added with a twinkle.

Each of the children was given an allowance of money before they set off gaily to find Cherry.

So as not to get lost in the crowds of people, the twins held hands. Freddie and Flossie broke away occasionally, but Nan kept them in sight at all times.

"The sign says this way to Loony Lane," Bert said presently.

When they reached it, they noticed that Loony Lane was very narrow and decorated with clown flags. Flossie stopped beside a funny-looking bench shaped like a shoe. A voice seemed to come out of the bench. "Sit down, little girl, sit down!"

Flossie carefully sat on it. As she did, a loud horn sound was heard. She jumped up, startled, and the voice said, "I'm a shoe horn! Listen to me blow!"

"That was fun!" Flossie said.

Up ahead the children saw a gift shop and Nan said, "Let's buy something for Mother and Daddy."

"Okay," the others agreed.

Now the sidewalk led beneath a big fake tree.

As the children filed under it, a rubbery limb tapped them on the shoulder and the tree said, "May I hold your coat? I'm a clothes tree!"

The twins laughed and scooted out of the way.

"I thought that tree was going to catch me!" Freddie chuckled.

They entered the gift shop and looked about, trying to find something suitable for their parents.

"I think this would be nice," Flossie said. She had picked out a pillow with *World of Fun* stitched on it in bright colors.

"I like it, too," said Freddie. "It would look nice on our sofa."

Bert found a gift he thought his father would like. It was a gold-colored necktie, and on it were the words "Number One Daddy."

They made the purchases and the clerk put the pillow and the tie into a shopping bag.

"I'll carry it," Bert offered. They walked on through Loony Lane, and Freddie spied a little automobile. A sign said, "Ride me!"

He slipped into the driver's seat, and immediately the car began to wiggle and jiggle. Then it said, "Get off! Get off, you're tickling me!"

Freddie jumped off like a flash and the laughing children continued on.

Flossie was now in the lead, and a group of

"May I hold your coat? I'm a clothes tree!"

animal clowns danced around. One of them, an Ugly Duckling, put his arms around the little girl. His beak came close to Flossie's head and whispered, "Watch out, you're being followed!"

Then the Ugly Duckling waddled off, while Flossie raced to tell the others.

"Do you suppose it was a joke?" asked Nan.

"I don't know," Bert said.

They looked all around them to see if any other person was observing them.

"Nothing but a chipmunk and a mouse," Nan said.

The two animal clowns seemed to stare for a moment, but then scampered off into the crowd.

"Well, let's find Cherry," Bert said.

At the end of Loony Lane was a path leading to the seaplane dock. A sign announced the schedule of takeoffs and Nan said, "The plane will leave in a few minutes. Come on, hurry!"

The children ran down to the plane, where half a dozen passengers were boarding. Standing near the door was a person whose clown suit was identical to the airplane itself.

The clown had a skin head that nearly came to a point, topped by a little propeller. Most of her face was chalk white, except for black triangle eyebrows, a purple nose, and a large orange-colored mouth. It curved up and made the Flying Clown appear to be laughing all the time.

"That must be Cherry," Bert said. "She sure looks funny."

At that moment there was a loud bang. It came from the side of the dock near the plane and was followed by billowing black smoke. The passengers who were already inside the craft hurried out in fright.

"I want a refund!" a woman demanded.

"You're right," a man agreed with her. "It's a good thing that bomb didn't go off inside the plane."

Soon all of the passengers were out. With worried faces they made their way to the nearby ticket booth to get their money back.

By this time the smoke bomb had fizzled out and two cowboys rushed up to investigate the trouble.

"Another mean trick!" the Flying Clown said aloud.

"Are you Cherry?" Nan asked her.

"Yes. Do you children want to go for a ride? I lost all my other passengers."

The Bobbseys pulled their money out and counted it. But they had spent too much in the gift shop.

"We'll come back and ride your plane another time," Nan said. "Right now we want to ask you some questions about Howie." She introduced herself and her brothers and sister and told about the phone call and the incident at the pool.

The Flying Clown's happy mouth seemed to droop at the corners. "Is my brother all right? Has anything happened to him?"

"Not that we know of," Nan said.

"I'm so worried," Cherry said. "Let's sit inside the plane and talk."

The Bobbseys climbed into the comfortable seats. Cherry said that she and Howie had been alone in the world since the death of their parents several years before.

"My father was a pilot and taught me how to fly," Cherry said. "After my parents died we got a trailer and moved from place to place. It was then that I decided to become an aerial clown. It's my life's ambition. We came to Florida and I enrolled in the clown school. Winter quarters of the Jumbo Circus are near here, you know."

Tears welled up in the girl's eyes. "But I had a terrible experience. I was getting along so well in my trapeze work. Then strange things began to happen."

"Like what?" Bert asked.

"My costumes were stolen one night. Then

somebody smeared paint on the windows of our trailer. And Old Man River kept begging me to give up clown school."

"Who's he?" Flossie wanted to know.

"His real name was George Rivero. He was an old clown and felt girls should stay away from that profession. Everywhere I went Mr. Rivero would say, 'Don't be an aerial clown! Don't be an aerial clown!' "   . .

"Well, you didn't leave just for that reason, did you?" Nan said.

"No. It was on account of another clown, Horsey Raines. I didn't trust him. One day I saw him pick the pocket of a clown school visitor!"

"What a bad man!" Flossie exclaimed.

"Why'd they call him Horsey?" Bert asked. "Did he ride horses?"

Cherry smiled. "No. It was because he was very odd looking—sort of a horse face." She described the man, with his long chin, high forehead, and stick-out ears.

"What about a scar?" Bert asked, excitement in his voice.

"Oh, yes, he had a scar. How do you know?"

"Because he may have been the man who chased Howie around the pool! Horsey Raines may be right here at the World of Fun!"

CHAPTER V

PEANUT POWER

"WE can't say for sure that it was Horsey," Cherry said. "It may be a coincidence. But do you know what? Horsey never liked Howie."

"I think there's more to it than that," Nan reasoned. "If Horsey is stealing things from the World of Fun and Howie knows about it, Horsey might be afraid he'll tell the police!"

"I don't think he'd do that," Cherry said. "He's afraid of policemen ever since I was accused in clown school."

The Bobbseys were eager to hear what had happened while Cherry was learning to become a clown.

She said, "After I told the manager that

Horsey was a pickpocket, Horsey denied it. A few days later the cash box was stolen. Everybody made a big search, and it was found under my bed—empty!"

"Surely nobody believed you did it!" Nan protested.

"The police came and asked me lots of questions," Cherry went on. She explained that nearly everyone at clown school thought that the real thief had hidden the cash box under her bed to put the blame on her.

"But there was always some doubt," she concluded. "I couldn't work in such an unpleasant place, so I left."

"But you did learn lots about being a flying clown, didn't you?" Freddie asked.

"Oh, yes. I know about makeup and costumes and acrobatics. But there are many tricks that I've never had a chance to practice."

The Bobbseys felt sorry for all the trouble Cherry was having.

"We're going to find Howie for you even if we have to stay here all year!" Freddie declared.

"If we only knew where to start looking!" Nan said.

"I know," Cherry replied. "On Zoo Island. He loves it and might visit now and then. I've been going over there myself whenever I can; but I've never caught him." She pointed to a small island, no larger than a city block, which was connected to the mainland by a narrow walkway.

"Oh, goody!" Flossie said, jumping up and down. "Let's go right now and find a clue!"

The others agreed and Cherry gave them her address and telephone number. They promised to get in touch with her if they learned anything new about Howie.

Before they left, Nan asked, "Cherry, why is Howie such a poor speller?"

"He changed schools several times and missed a lot of days. I guess that's why."

Freddie and Flossie skipped on ahead and Flossie bought a bag of peanuts at a refreshment stand. While the younger twins munched on the nuts, Bert and Nan talked more about the mystery.

"If that man was Horsey Raines, and if we're trying to help Howie, Horsey will be after us, too!" Nan reasoned.

"Maybe that's what the Ugly Duckling's warning was all about," Bert said.

"I'll bet it was Howie in one of his disguises," Nan said. "Flossie should have tried to catch him."

They had just passed the Safari Trading Post near the entrance to Zoo Island when they noticed a commotion on the narrow bridge. People were shouting and grabbing at something which darted between their legs and over their shoulders.

"It looks like a little girl in a pink dress," Flossie said. "My goodness, she's a fast runner!"

"That's no little girl," Bert told her. "It's a baby chimpanzee!"

"Catch her when she tries to get past us," Freddie said.

The frightened little animal came closest to Nan. The girl reached over to grab her, but only got one hand on a furry leg. The animal blinked her brown eyes, wrinkled her nose, and zipped away in an instant.

"Catch her! Catch her!" called a man in a white uniform. "Catch Lulu!"

"He must be the zoo keeper," Bert said, and the Bobbseys took off after the chimp.

A child was just coming out of the Safari Trading Post. Lulu quickly dashed in through the open door. Customers gasped in surprise as the animal started climbing up the shelves.

When people reached out for her, Lulu dropped gifts on them—coconut shells, wooden bowls, grass skirts. Then she found an explorer's pith helmet and put it on her head. This made everyone laugh.

"The poor thing, she's so frightened," Flossie said. "Here, Lulu, come to me!" She reached her chubby arms toward the runaway.

The manager of the Safari Trading Post was growing angry. "She's ruining my shop!" he complained. "Lulu, stay away from these expensive blown-glass gifts!"

But Lulu paid no attention to him. Her furry paws reached for a few glass ornaments and dropped them to the floor with a tinkling crash.

Then she grabbed a beautiful multicolored fish.

"No! Don't throw that!" the man cried.

But Lulu did. As the souvenir sailed through the air, Bert leaped forward and caught it before it hit the floor. He returned it to the manager.

"Thank you, young man," he said, relieved. "This is worth a lot of money!"

Now the onlookers were laughing and shouting to Lulu. Then the zoo keeper's voice sounded above the turmoil. "Please, everybody be quiet! You're scaring the little chimp!"

A hush came over the store while the man talked calmly to Lulu. She looked down at him, scratched herself, and made funny faces by raising her upper lip.

Suddenly Flossie's tiny voice was heard. "Lulu, please come to me! I won't hurt you."

Lulu gazed at her, made more silly faces, and came one shelf lower.

"No! Don't throw that!" the man cried.

"That's right, honey," Flossie urged. "If you make it all the way, I'll give you a peanut!" She held one toward Lulu.

Everyone stood in silence when, like a brown blur, Lulu jumped into Flossie's outstretched arms!

Bert, who stood behind his sister, prevented both of them from tumbling to the floor. "That's what you call peanut power!" He chuckled.

Happily eating the peanuts with one hand, Lulu clung to Flossie with the other.

"This way!" the zoo keeper ordered. "Take her back to Zoo Island, little girl."

The customers made a path for Flossie and Lulu, and they went out the door, followed by the other twins.

Zoo Island was beautiful. Except for the aviaries for small birds, there were no cages or fences. The animals roamed around free on various small islands surrounded by moats. From a distance it looked as if they were all together in one place. Some very tame species walked around freely among the visitors, and children were allowed to pet them.

Flossie did not want Lulu to go back, but the zoo keeper explained that she must be returned to her mother. He thanked Flossie for her help and took the little animal to her family group.

Then the girls wandered off together, while Bert and Freddie walked into a palm grove. They heard someone shouting, "Git up! Git up!"

"They must have horses here, too," Freddie said, and dashed on ahead. Then he turned and called back, "Hey, Bert, it's not a horse. It's a big turtle!"

When Bert caught up with his brother, he saw a boy about his own age riding on a giant turtle. He wore a sweatshirt with the name Randy across the front. The boy had a stick and was pounding the shellback.

Bert ran up to him. "Don't beat the turtle like that!" he said angrily. "You might hurt him!"

"Oh, he's got a thick shell and won't mind," Randy replied.

The turtle had pulled in his head and claws, and with the tip of his nose he peeked out again. The boy whacked it.

"Here, hold this," Bert said and gave the shopping bag to Freddie. Then he jumped up on top of the turtle and knocked Randy down.

"Oh, you want a fight, eh?" the boy sneered.

"I just want to get you off that turtle!"

The loud voices had drawn the attention of passersby, including several animal clowns. A Baby Bear sidled up to Freddie and asked what

all the fuss was about. Just then Randy punched
Bert, and Bert punched him back.

Soon they were wrestling on the ground, roll-
ing over and over.

"That's enough! Stop it!" shouted a deep
voice. A cowboy stepped through the crowd
surrounding the fighting children and hauled
both to their feet.

"He was hitting the turtle," Bert explained.

"Don't ever do that again!" the cowboy told
Randy. Then he turned to Bert. "Where's that
shopping bag you were carrying?"

Bert was dumbfounded at the question. He
looked around and spied Freddie. "My brother
has it," he said. "Why do you ask?"

The cowboy strode over to Freddie and
looked into the bag. "So that man was right!"
he said. The officer put his hand inside, and
pulled out two beautiful crystal birds.

"These were stolen from the Safari Trading
Post!" he said sternly. "Come with me!"

CHAPTER VI

MOON DOGS

"THERE's been a mistake!" Bert told the officer. "Those birds don't belong to us!"

"I'll say they don't!" the cowboy replied. "There's been a lot of shoplifting going on in the World of Fun."

"Shoplifting!" Bert exclaimed. "We wouldn't do such a thing!"

"Sure. The birds flew into your bag by themselves."

The onlookers seemed just as surprised as the Bobbseys. One gray-haired woman shook her head and said, "You can never tell these days just by the way people look."

Another remarked, "I wonder if the parents know what their children are up to!"

Just then Nan and Flossie walked up and inquired about what had happened. When Bert told them, Nan's face flushed with embarrassment and hot tears welled into her eyes. "Somebody's trying to frame us!" she told the policeman. "Pete Prescott will tell you that we're not thieves!"

"Oh, you know the chief? Well, we'll see if you're telling the truth. Come on, now, all four of you!" As they walked off, the boy Bert had been fighting with snickered, and Bert felt like punching him again.

Nearing the bridge, the cowboy pulled a walkie-talkie from his belt, spoke to headquarters, and asked for the chief.

The Bobbseys heard the reply. "He's not here. Any message?"

"Tell him I've got four kids with some stolen goods. Send a wagon to Zoo Island."

In a few minutes a little car designed to resemble a chuck wagon arrived and the Bobbseys were ordered inside. "And don't try to jump out!" the officer warned. Flossie started to cry.

When they arrived at the Gingerbread Castle, the cowboy led them into the chief's office. Pete had returned and was sitting behind his desk.

"Well, the Bobbseys!" he said, standing up to greet them. "What can I do for you?"

"You can tell this officer that we're not thieves!" Bert said.

"Thieves? What do you mean?"

The cowboy told what happened. "A man reported to me that the children stole gifts at the Safari Trading Post during the chimpanzee commotion and I found some in their bag."

"That man was one of the real thieves," Nan declared. "You should have caught *him!*"

"I wanted him to come along," the cowboy said, "but when I turned around he was gone."

"What did he look like?" Pete asked.

"He was tall and wiry, and his arms were covered with tattoos."

Pete was sorry about the incident and told the officer that he had done his duty, but had been fooled by the man. He gave orders to pass on the description of the fellow to all cowboys and to be on the lookout for him.

To the Bobbseys he said, "If you ever need me, dial Number 3 from any telephone. It's the direct line to my office." Then, seeing that Flossie's eyes were red from crying, he lifted her to his shoulders and said, "How about having lunch with me? I know a good place."

"Where?" Freddie asked, and Flossie brightened.

"You'll see, just come with me."

Nan said good-by to the cowboy and told him

not to feel too bad. "But please catch that man," she said. "He's mean!"

The children flocked around Pete as he led them down the street and past the Rainbow Novelty Shop. Then he turned left on another street. Halfway along, the children spied what looked like a Ferris wheel lying on its side. A sign above it read: Outer Space Wheel.

"It's really a restaurant," Pete explained. "It revolves slowly and you can see a lot of things while you're having lunch."

The children walked into the space wheel, found a table on the outside wall, and sat down. A waiter, dressed like a Martian with antennas sticking out of his head, handed them menus.

"Look, they have Moon Dogs," Bert said, laughing. "What are they?" he asked the waiter.

"Something like a hot dog, but bigger," the man replied.

"I want a Moon Dog! I want a Moon Dog!" said Freddie.

"Me, too!" the other children chorused.

"Include me," said Pete. "That'll be five Moon Dogs. And would you like sodas and ice cream?"

The twins said yes and the Martian hurried off to get their orders. While they were waiting, they talked about the trick that had been played on them.

"Look, they have Moon Dogs," Bert said.

"Somebody wants to embarrass you and perhaps make you leave the World of Fun," Pete said.

"But we won't!" Freddie declared. "Not until we find Howie!"

"That might be the reason behind all this," Pete said. "I hope we can find that man and straighten things out."

"But what about Cherry and Horsey Raines?" Bert asked.

"I've been thinking about that," Pete said. "If Raines works for the circus, how could he be doing mischief at the World of Fun? And how could he chase Howie around at night? That's when they perform!"

"Maybe he's not there any more," Nan said.

"We'd better find out," Pete said. "I don't want any harm to come to Howie."

"Perhaps Cherry could take us to the circus," Bert suggested. "It's not too far from here."

"I understand they'll be leaving on tour in a few days," the chief said. "You'll have to hurry up."

Just then the waiter arrived with the Moon Dogs. Each of the big sausages was cradled in a fat roll. Freddie tried to stuff one end into his mouth, but it wouldn't open wide enough.

The others laughed and Nan said, "You'll have to nibble on it, Freddie."

After they had finished, Freddie asked Pete, "Now can we see the underworld?"

"That's exactly what we'll do. But before I take you there, how would you like to see the brain of the World of Fun?" He pointed to the Magic Mountain, where steaming red smoke was rising from the volcano. Halfway down, a waterfall sprang out from the side, cascading to a large pool below.

"Water is pumped to a trough up there," Pete explained. "Follow me and I'll show you."

He opened a door at the base of the mountain and they went inside. At the end of a short corridor was an elevator. They entered and rode up what seemed to be several stories.

There the door opened into a large, brightly lighted room. In it were a computer and several banks of instrument panels. High on the wall were a number of television screens. A dozen employees were busy watching the screens and the instrument panels.

"Everything in the World of Fun is controlled right from this room," Pete said. "We can stop or start any of the amusements, turn off the falls, or hold the monorail."

"What are the TV's for?" Flossie asked.

"That's so we can get a good look at all parts of the park," Pete replied.

The children's eyes roved from screen to

screen. They saw people coming out of boats after riding the rapids in Davy Jones's Locker. They noticed Cherry's airplane coming in for a landing. The monorail station and the ticket booth at the entrance to World of Fun could also be seen.

"Now we'll take the elevator down into the underground," Pete said.

"First, will you show us how the water spills out of the mountain?" Freddie asked.

"Of course. That's up higher, next to the last stop of the elevator."

"What's the last one?" Flossie asked.

"The fireworks room. Visitors aren't allowed there."

They returned to the elevator and rode up to the next stop. There they stepped into a dim narrow room. It smelled cool and damp. Below the floor level was a long deep trough, guarded on either side by a railing. At one end, water gurgled up from a big pipe. It filled the trough and ran swiftly to a hole in the side of the Magic Mountain, where it fell far down into a canal.

"We usually don't let visitors in here, either," Pete said. "You can see how dangerous it could be."

"It's scary," Nan said, looking through the hole to the blue sky outside.

"All right, let's go downstairs now," Pete said, and turned toward the door.

At that moment Freddie leaned far over the railing.

"Don't do that!" Bert called out. He grabbed for his brother, but his foot slipped on the damp floor.

Bert skidded under the railing and splashed into the swiftly running water!

CHAPTER VII

THE HIDING PLACE

THE frightened children screamed while Bert thrashed about in the water. Pete dashed to the wall and threw a switch. As if by magic, the water ceased to flow!

It became smooth and still. The security chief stood for a moment, his face quite pale, mopping his brow with a handkerchief.

"I was afraid you might go over before I could turn off the water," he said shakily.

"I'm okay," Bert called out and swam back. Suddenly his right foot touched an object in the bottom of the trough. "Hey, Pete, something's in here!" he said.

"There shouldn't be. Find out what it is."

Bert searched underwater with his hands and popped to the surface again. "It's a big heavy sack," he reported. "I don't think I can move it by myself!"

"Wait a minute, I'll help," Pete said. He slipped off his loafers, climbed over the rail and jumped into the trough. Then he and Bert tugged at the sack. They hauled it out and took the elevator back to the computer room.

Several of the employees gathered to look at their find.

"It's waterproof," Pete noted as he untied the bag. Then he turned it upside down.

Dozens of souvenirs spilled out onto the floor!

"The loot! It's the loot!" Nan cried out. "Look! These might be the Swiss watches stolen from the Rainbow Novelty Shop!"

"Well, I'll be a monkey's uncle!" Pete said. "Bert, you found the hiding place used by the thieves!"

The boy grinned. "Yes, but Freddie helped me."

"How?" Pete asked.

"By making me fall in!"

The twins examined the beautiful trinkets.

"They're all high-priced items," Pete said. "I wonder what made them think of such a good hiding place."

"It's the loot!" Nan cried out.

"Is there another way to get up here?" Bert asked.

"No," Pete replied. "The thieves had to take the elevator."

"Maybe they're workers at the World of Fun," Nan said.

The chief said that all employees had been investigated thoroughly. Besides, the control center was heavily guarded, and people had to check in and out by showing their identification tags.

Freddie tried to look important. "Well, there must be a bad apple in the barrel somewhere," he said.

"I'm afraid so," Pete admitted. "And I'll find out who it is, too!"

He called one of his security men and asked him to return the souvenirs to their rightful owners. Then everyone took the elevator down and walked outside.

"We'll have to postpone our visit to the 'underworld,'" Pete said. "I have to change my clothes. But I promise we'll do it soon."

With Nan carrying the shopping bag, the children started back to their motel. On the way Freddie and Flossie stopped first for spun taffy then for candy bars.

"I think you're eating too many sweets," Nan

warned. "Peanuts this morning, ice cream, and now all this. You'll get sick!"

"No, we won't," Flossie assured her. She wrinkled her nose, licked her lips, and bit into the nuts and chocolate. "Mmm-m, yummy, this is good!"

When they arrived at the African Village, they found their parents sitting beside the pool in swimsuits.

"Did you beat Daddy at golf?" Nan asked as she ran up to hug her mother.

"She sure did," Mr. Bobbsey said. "But next time *I'll* win!"

Then Nan made her parents close their eyes and hold out their hands. She gave the pillow to her mother and the tie to her father.

"Now you can look!" Flossie said with a giggle.

"Oh, what beautiful gifts!" Mrs. Bobbsey exclaimed.

"I'll wear the tie at dinner tonight," Mr. Bobbsey said.

While the younger twins raced off to get their bathing suits, Bert and Nan recounted all the exciting adventures of the day.

"My goodness!" their mother said. "You've certainly been busy detectives!"

"I wonder how long the thieves meant to keep that loot hidden?" Mr. Bobbsey said.

"Probably until the heat was off," Bert suggested. Then he turned to his sister. "Come on, let's get ready for the pool."

It was not long before all six Bobbseys were splashing about in the water. After the refreshing dip they went in to dress for dinner.

"May we invite Cherry to eat with us?" Nan asked.

"Of course," her mother said. "Call her up. Daddy and I would like to meet her."

"Maybe we can visit the clown school with her to check on Horsey Raines," Bert said.

When Cherry arrived shortly before seven, none of the children recognized her. She introduced herself and Bert said, "I can't believe it. You don't look the same at all. Are you really the Flying Clown?"

"Cross my heart," Cherry said, tossing her long blond hair. "The clown face makes me look altogether different, doesn't it?"

"It sure does. Now you're very pretty," Flossie spoke up. Everyone laughed.

At dinner Freddie and Flossie did not eat much at all.

"What's the matter with you?" Mrs. Bobbsey asked. "You're just picking at your food!"

Bert and Nan looked at each other knowingly.

"It must be the heat," Flossie said sweetly,

and nobody mentioned the goodies they had eaten.

Conversation turned to Howie and all the troubles he and Cherry had had.

Mrs. Bobbsey said, "We understand that Horsey Raines might be prowling around the World of Fun."

"We'll have to find out for sure," Bert said. "Cherry, could you take us to the circus so we can see if Horsey is really the man who chased Howie?"

"I'll be glad to. The weather forecast for tomorrow is rain. If it's too bad for flying, we'll go."

After the meal they strolled about the African Village for a while, then Cherry said good night and drove back to her trailer.

The Bobbseys awakened next morning to hear the wind whistling through the palmettos. The sky was dark and cloudy, and even before breakfast it began to rain heavily.

"Good," Bert thought. "Maybe we can visit the circus today."

When he roused Freddie to get up, his brother had a sad look on his face. "Bert, I don't feel well," he said. "My stomach hurts."

Nan knocked on the door a few minutes later to report that Flossie didn't want any breakfast either.

When Mrs. Bobbsey came in and was told

about the condition of the younger twins, she said, "Nan, Bert, you run along and have breakfast with Daddy. I'll take care of these two rascals. It's probably no more than an overdose of sweets."

Freddie grinned sheepishly. "How did you know?"

At breakfast Bert and Nan were interrupted by a phone call from Cherry. "I can't fly today. Would you like to go to the circus and the clown school?"

"We sure would," Nan said, but explained that only she and Bert would be going.

"Okay. I'll pick you up around noon."

Wearing light transparent raincoats, Nan and Bert met Cherry in front of their huts when she arrived. It was about an hour's drive to the circus, and Bert was nearly lulled to sleep by the gentle clicketyclack of the windshield wiper and the whisper of the tires on the wet pavement.

"Here we are," Cherry said finally, pulling into a large field. In the center stood an enormous circus tent. On the grounds were animal cages on wheels and a number of trailers which Cherry said were used for living quarters. A railroad siding was nearby.

She parked the car and the trio walked toward the entrance.

"Do you have any plan for your sleuthing?"

Cherry asked the youngsters, as she wiped raindrops from her face.

"Yes," Bert replied. "Besides seeing Horsey Raines, I want to ask Old Man River a few questions."

An attendant at the door recognized Cherry and let the three inside. Bert and Nan looked up in awe to see four aerialists practicing high above the center ring.

Off to one side five elephants were being led away by an old man.

"That's Mr. Rivero," Cherry said. "But what's he doing with elephants? He hardly knows anything about them!"

She asked one of the roustabouts how long the clown had been working with the pachyderms. She was told that the trainer had been ill for a few days and the job of tending to the big animals had been left to Old Man River.

"One of those elephants is a mean actor," Cherry said. "I hope Mr. Rivero knows how to handle Oscar!"

The huge beasts seemed to be moving in slow motion, and as they came closer, the largest one stopped.

"Come on, Oscar, on your way!" the old man ordered. He tapped the elephant with a pole. Oscar swung around and before Old Man River could run, he encircled him with his trunk, lifted him high into the air, then dropped him to the ground!

"Stop! Stop!" Cherry screamed. She ran forward, with Bert and Nan at her heels. Just then the angry beast trumpeted loudly and reared up on his hind legs!

CHAPTER VIII

THE BROWN PACKAGE

NAN and Cherry screamed for help and all three rushed toward the elephant. He was standing on his hind legs, trunk swinging back and forth.

Bert and Nan reached the injured clown and with the help of Cherry pulled him out of the way just before the elephant's huge feet clomped to the ground.

Mr. Rivero was carried another twenty feet along the sawdust while half a dozen roustabouts corraled big Oscar.

"He's still conscious," Cherry said. "We must get him to the infirmary quickly!"

The other circus people seemed to know how to handle an emergency situation. Along came two clowns riding in a small car. They gently picked up the injured man and sped out of the big top to a nearby trailer.

Nan, Bert, and Cherry watched as Old Man River was carried into the circus hospital. He was given first aid by two other clowns, who were especially trained for this, and fifteen minutes later a local doctor hurried in.

The three rescuers waited in the rain until the physician appeared.

"How is he?" Cherry asked anxiously.

"No broken bones," the doctor said. "But he's badly shaken up and has a slight concussion. You can talk to him if you want, but not for long, please!"

They found Old Man River on a neat, white cot with a bandage wrapped around his head. Seeing Cherry, he turned his eyes to one side and would not look at her directly.

A tear ran down beside the clown's nose, and Cherry bent over to wipe it with a tissue.

"I'm not mad at you," she said. "Everything that's past is past. But some day, Mr. Rivero, will you tell me why you don't want me to become an aerial clown?"

The old man did not reply. Instead, he closed his eyes.

The two other clowns motioned to the visitors that he should be left alone now. The

Bobbseys and Cherry said good-by and walked out into the drizzle.

"Mr. Rivero seemed to be awfully sorry about something," Nan remarked.

"But why?" Cherry asked, shaking her head. "Oh, I wish I knew."

"Shall we go check on Horsey now?" Bert said.

"Yes," Cherry replied. "There's his trailer."

A sign over the door read: Raines.

Cherry knocked on the door. No answer.

Bert put his ear against it to listen. "I hear somebody stirring!" the boy declared.

Nan knocked again while Bert walked around the side and looked in a window. When he came back he said, "A man's lying on a bunk."

"Do you suppose something's wrong with Horsey Raines?" Nan wondered.

"Let's see," Cherry said. She tried the handle and the door opened. "Horsey, are you all right?" she called out.

Still no reply. She walked in and shook the man's shoulder. He turned over, bleary-eyed, and gazed up at her.

"Molo!" Cherry exclaimed.

"What are you doing here?" the man demanded. He sat up and threw his feet over the side of the bunk.

"I'm sorry. We thought you were Horsey and didn't feel well."

"Horsey's not here," Molo said in a surly tone. "What do you want him for, anyway? And who are these kids?"

A bit flustered, Cherry made the introductions. "They're friends of mine and visiting in Florida," she said and explained to the twins that Molo was a retired clown and friend of Horsey's.

"Where is Mr. Raines?" Nan asked.

"None of your business," Molo replied. He sniffed several times and his bloodshot eyes regarded his visitors suspiciously. "This ain't no social call, is it?"

"Not exactly," Cherry said. "We just wanted to tell Horsey that Old Man River has been hurt by Oscar."

"That mean old elephant!" Molo said. "He hurt me once, too."

"Will you tell Horsey about it when he comes back?" Cherry said.

"He ain't coming back for some time."

"He isn't? Why not?"

"He went to Chicago," Molo said. "Been gone about a month to visit his sick brother." He noticed a look of doubt on Cherry's face. "You don't believe me, eh? Well, here's a letter he sent. Look at the postmark. Chicago!"

Cherry glanced at it, nodded her head, and said, "Bert and Nan wanted to meet Horsey. Do you have a photo of him?"

"Oh, circus fans, eh?" Molo warmed up a little to his visitors. "Yeah, there's a picture around here somewhere, on a poster." He got up and rummaged around through a stack of papers on a table at the end of the trailer.

"Here it is," he said and handed the poster to Nan.

A look of fright came over the girl's face. She showed the picture to her brother. It was the man they had seen at the pool!

"Thank you," Bert said and gave the poster back to Molo. Then they said good-by and left.

Outside the twins jabbered excitedly.

"Horsey's the one!" Nan said. "I'm sure of it!"

"He's trying to get Howie!" Bert said. "He's not in Chicago, he's at the World of Fun!"

They started to walk away, when Cherry pointed to another circus trailer some distance from Horsey's.

"There's where I stayed when I attended clown school," she said. "It was so cozy, Nan. I fixed it up real cute. See the plaid curtains in the window? I made them."

"Do you think we can peek inside?" Nan asked.

"If nobody lives there now, we could. I'll ask."

She walked up to a pleasant-looking woman, spoke a few words, then returned.

"That was Zelda the snake charmer," Cherry explained. "She said nobody has lived in the trailer since I left. It's open, so let's go in."

While Cherry and Nan chatted, Bert parted the curtains and gazed out the window across the rainy circus grounds. "Look here!" he said.

Nan and Cherry hurried beside him to see the door to Horsey's trailer open slowly. Out came Molo, dressed in raincoat and rainhat. Under his arm he carried a brown package tied with red string. He looked about cautiously, then made his way to a phone booth. After talking for a few minutes, he went to a blue car parked nearby and drove off.

"I wonder what he's up to," Bert said. "He looked suspicious."

"Let's follow him," Cherry suggested. "Come on, hurry!"

Their shoes soggy with mud and rain, the trio raced to Cherry's car and climbed in. She drove down the highway with Molo in sight, but careful not to get too close.

Finally they reached an intersection in the highway. A big sign on the left said: Visit the Alligator Farm.

"Let's follow him," Cherry suggested.

Molo turned and Cherry said, "This is the road that goes past the trailer camp where I live."

They continued on for a while, and presently a big flatbed truck approached them. It was carrying a house trailer. Red flags on either side of the load warned oncoming traffic to give it a wide berth.

"I wish that driver would get over and let me have some room," Cherry complained. She pulled to the side as far as she could.

"Watch out!" Bert shouted.

Cherry reacted by turning left, and the right front wheel skidded into a ditch filled with rain water. They teetered dangerously to one side.

"Oh, dear!" Cherry said. She spun the wheel, but was unable to get out of the mud.

Molo was out of sight by now.

"What bad luck!" Nan said. "What'll we do about it, Cherry?"

"You stay here with Bert while I go for help," Cherry said. "Turn on the radio to entertain yourselves."

Cherry thumbed a ride to find the closest garage, and Bert flicked on the radio. The first thing they heard was a weather report. No letup in the storm! It was expected to last till the next morning.

This was followed by a bulletin. The announcer said, "Warning to all people in the area. The alligator farm has been flooded out and many of the creatures have escaped. Most of them are small, but two large ones got away and could be dangerous!"

Nan shuddered. "I wouldn't want one of those things to bite me!" she said.

"It wouldn't just bite," Bert declared. "It would eat you up!"

"You can't scare me!" Nan said stoutly.

As the radio station played hit songs, the twins wondered how long it would take for Cherry to get help. Nan glanced at the rear-view mirror, hoping to see a tow truck come along at any moment. Suddenly she cried out, "Bert, look!"

"What?"

"Alligators! In the ditch!"

Bert turned around to see two small snouts some distance away. They approached slowly.

"The police should know about this!" Bert said. "I'm going to tell the next car that passes."

"Please be careful," Nan said as her brother wriggled out the door at the driver's side.

"Don't worry!" He waved his hands and stopped the first car that came along.

"Two alligators are in the ditch," he told the man at the wheel. "Will you get word to the police?"

"Right away, son. Thanks for the tip."

The car drove away and Bert turned to get back to Nan. But as he did, a huge long snout with reptilian eyes poked out from under Cherry's sedan. Bert jumped back in fright!

CHAPTER IX

A MIDNIGHT PROWLER

WHEN Nan saw how frightened her brother looked, she called out, "What's the matter, Bert?"

"There's a big alligator under the car."

Nan clapped a hand to her mouth in alarm. "Oh, Bert! Watch out!"

The boy ran to the other side of the road and picked up a long stick. With it he whacked the alligator on the snout. The big beast backed off and Nan saw the long, slimy tail as it disappeared into the muddy water of the ditch.

Bert hopped into the car and slammed the door. "Look, Nan. It's swimming away," he said.

Shortly afterward Cherry returned, riding in the front seat of a tow truck. Following her was a police car with several men. They went after the alligators with long poles and lassos.

The fellow in the tow truck attached a chain to the front of Cherry's car and slowly pulled it out onto the road.

The girl laughed and said, "I didn't expect to have so much excitement when I took you to the circus grounds."

As she paid the garage man, Nan said, "What now, Cherry?"

"We'll drive home."

They had gone only a few miles when another bulletin came over the radio. The storm had become more severe. Motorists were advised to stay off the roads if at all possible.

"I have an idea," Cherry said. "I'll drive to my trailer and phone your parents. Perhaps you can stay overnight with me."

"Oh, great!" Nan said. "A slumber party!"

Cherry smiled. "Bert, you don't mind coming to a slumber party, do you?"

"Not if there's only *two* girls!"

The rain fell in torrents and Cherry had to drive very slowly. Finally she said, "There's my camp. Welcome to Sunny Vista."

She pulled up beside a trailer. Its base was enclosed by white wooden lattice work. On either side of the door was a small strip of flower garden bordered by a low picket fence.

"Hurry up before you get drowned!" Cherry said. She stepped out of the car and opened the door. When the children had entered, Bert said, "Hey, this is neat!"

Two bunk beds occupied the far wall of the cozy dwelling. Next to them stood a table with benches.

"And here's my little kitchen," Cherry said, pointing to the other end. "Goodness, what's this?"

On a plate beside the sink were several chicken bones and next to it was a glass with some milk still in it.

"Somebody's been here and raided the refrigerator!" Cherry declared. "Oh, that brother of mine! Why didn't he stay?"

"Are you sure it was Howie?" Nan asked.

"Almost certain," Cherry replied. She searched around for some kind of message which Howie might have left. Then she noticed the top of his built-in dresser. "His marbles are gone!" she said. "See, it *was* Howie."

She told the Bobbseys that Howie had a hobby of collecting antique marbles which he kept in a leather sack. It had been on the dresser that morning.

"Let's look for more clues," Nan suggested,

and all three of them investigated every nook and cranny in the trailer.

Finally Nan found a piece of paper under the pillow of Cherry's bunk bed.

"I found something!" she called out.

Cherry and Bert looked over her shoulder as she read the message. "Bad guys furius becuz loot was stole. Warn the Bobsies and don't worry about me."

"Good night!" Bert said. "They must have returned to the Magic Mountain for the waterproof sack."

"I'm sure they're angry because they were outwitted," Cherry said. "Maybe they even think Howie took it!"

"Let's call Mom and Dad and warn them about the thieves," Bert suggested.

Nan went to the telephone and told her parents what had happend.

Mrs. Bobbsey said they would be very careful and wished the twins a good night's sleep after their exciting day.

"How are Freddie and Flossie?" Nan asked.

"Fine. They've recovered from their 'sweet tummy'!"

Cherry and Nan prepared a delicious supper. Then the twins read magazines for a while before going to bed. The monotonous drumming of the rain on the roof lulled everyone to sleep, but in the middle of the night a flash of lightning and a thunderclap awakened Nan.

She got up quietly and looked out the window. There were more flashes far off in the distance. But then Nan saw a light close to the trailer.

"Somebody's walking with a flashlight," she told herself. Silently she tiptoed to Bert and woke him up.

"Sh-sh! Don't make any noise," she whispered, and reported what she had seen.

The twins slipped outside in their bare feet. The rainwater felt cool against their toes. Quietly they followed the person with the bobbing flashlight.

It was a man. He got into a car some distance from the trailer, started the motor, turned on the lights, and drove away.

"Bert? . . . Nan?" Cherry's voice came from the doorway. "Where are you?"

"Here!" Bert said. "We've been following a prowler. But he's gone now!"

"Come in, both of you, and get dried off!"

"Not yet, Cherry. We want to find out what the fellow was up to."

"Do you have a flashlight?" Nan asked.

"Yes. I'll bring it right out."

When Cherry returned with the light, Bert took it and began searching around the trailer.

Quietly they followed the person with the flashlight.

"What are you looking for?" Cherry asked.

"I don't know exactly," Bert said. "But that guy might have left a clue."

He and Nan circled the trailer several times, each time coming closer to it. Bert shone the light in the flower garden and felt among the blooms for anything the man might have dropped.

Then his beam followed the lattice work. At one point, near the back, was a small opening. The boy shone the light inside. At first all he saw were plumbing pipes.

Then his eyes fell on something. He reached in to pull out a brown bundle. It was wrapped tightly with red string!

"I found something!" he called out. "Let's go inside and see what it is."

He carried the package into the trailer and set it on the table.

"That looks like the same package Molo was carrying this afternoon!" Nan observed.

"But why would anyone put it under my place?" Cherry wondered.

"Maybe somebody's trying to frame you again, Cherry," Bert said. He untied the string carefully and opened the package. They gasped.

Inside were trinkets and souvenirs, most of them showing the initials W.O.F.

"Stolen from the World of Fun!" Nan said.

"But they won't put the blame on you again,

Cherry," Bert declared. "We'll see to that!"

The girl seemed stunned for a moment. Then she asked, "Do you suppose Molo brought that package here himself?"

"If not, he had somebody else do it for him," Bert guessed.

"Now what?" Nan asked. "Shall we turn it over to the police?"

"Not yet!" Cherry said with determination. "I'm going to take this package back to Mr. Molo and tell him a thing or two!"

She was really angry now, and Bert and Nan were a bit surprised. They had never seen Cherry like this before. But they realized that she had been persecuted long enough.

When they all had dressed, the Bobbseys hurried out to the car and Cherry closed the trailer door with a solid slam. "We'll see what Molo has to say when I confront him with the loot!" she said.

Cherry drove off into the night and nobody said another word until they reached the circus grounds. She parked the car a short distance from Molo's place.

"There's a light in his window," Nan observed as they approached cautiously. Nan carried the damp package and Cherry was just about to knock on the door when they heard muffled voices inside.

"We'll do the big job and clear out for Mexico as soon as it's finished," a man's voice said.

"Good idea. No more junk jewelry." This was Molo. "We've got a boatload of the stuff waiting for us on the island."

Silence for a few moments. Then a third voice hissed, "We've got to get those brats off our backs! Can you imagine? They found the stuff at the waterfall! Molo, did you drop off the package today?"

"Well, not exactly. There were people around. But I got my friend Muggsy to do it tonight. He's reliable."

"Then that gets Cherry out of the way."

Somebody moved inside. The door handle turned. Bert, Nan and Cherry scrambled to get out of the way as a crack of light shone through the darkness. The three huddled low behind the trailer.

"I—I dropped the package," Nan whispered. "It slipped from my fingers."

Just then an angry voice, like a lion's roar, shattered the stillness. "Molo! What does this mean? You dumbhead!"

CHAPTER X

A FOUR-BUTTON CLUE

BERT, Nan, and Cherry huddled behind the trailer, hardly daring to breathe. What if the angry man should find them?

The voices died down for a few moments, then flared up again.

"Molo, you lied! The package was never delivered! You ruined the whole deal!"

"Do you recognize who's talking?" Bert whispered to Cherry.

"No. Sh-sh!" she replied. "They might hear us."

The shouting stopped and the trio heard soggy footsteps going away from the trailer.

They peeked around the side to see two men disappearing into the darkness.

For a few moments someone walked about in the trailer, then the light blinked off and all was quiet.

Tiptoeing, Bert, Nan, and Cherry returned to the car and drove back to the girl's home.

"Molo got into trouble with his boss because I dropped the package," Nan said on the way.

"Serves him right!" Bert chuckled.

When they arrived, they noticed a police car next to Cherry's trailer. Its revolving light pulsed red in the darkness.

"I'm not surprised at this," Cherry said as they stepped out to confront an officer.

"Hello," she greeted him. "Is there something you are looking for?"

"Why, er, yes, as a matter of fact."

"Such as a package?"

"That's right. How did you know?"

Bert spoke up. "We just returned it to the man who sent it!"

"Oh, really?"

"You know who it is," Nan said. "Molo. He's the one who tipped you off, isn't he?"

The young policeman looked embarrassed and apologized for disturbing them. "I'll go see this Molo fellow," he declared, and drove away.

The Bobbseys had planned to get up early

next morning, but they overslept. By the time Cherry drove back to the World of Fun, it was mid-morning.

The rain had stopped and the sun was shining. Cherry dropped them off at the parking lot, then drove quickly to the dock to put on her makeup.

When Bert and Nan entered their huts, the rest of the family was gone. On Nan's dresser was a message written by her mother.

"Meet us at eleven at Davy Jones's Locker. Then we can all take the ride together."

Nan went to Bert's hut and showed him the note.

"Let's hurry," Bert said, "and catch up with them."

But before they had a chance to leave the African Village, they saw their mother, father, and Freddie hurrying toward them.

"Is she here? Did you see her?" Mrs. Bobbsey asked anxiously.

"See who?" Bert asked.

"Flossie, of course. We lost her somewhere along the way. And we thought maybe she had come back to the motel."

"She's not inside," Nan said.

The family searched around the pool and the children's playground. No Flossie.

Nan dialed Number 3 and talked with Pete.

"I'll have my men look for her," he said. "That makes the third lost child this morning. Would one of you like to stand by the TV monitors in the computer center? You may be able to spot Flossie more quickly than we can."

"I'll do it," Nan said.

"Okay. I'll tell them you're coming," the security chief said.

Nan reported the plan to her parents and hurried off.

Bert said, "Maybe Flossie went to Zoo Island to visit Lulu."

"That's possible," Mr. Bobbsey agreed. "Bert, why don't you go there while Mother and Freddie and I search around the place where we lost her."

They all went to the monorail station. Bert rode with his parents for a while, then got off at the stop nearest Zoo Island.

"I'll phone Pete if I find her," he said.

"Please do," Mrs. Bobbsey said. "I'm so worried since that gang of thieves threatened us."

The way to Zoo Island led past the airplane dock, where Cherry, with her clown makeup and propeller beanie, waited for passengers.

"Did Flossie come by here this morning?" Bert asked.

"No. Is there any problem?"

"She's lost. I didn't say anything to Mother

or Dad, but do you suppose she has been kidnapped?"

"Oh, dear!" Cherry said. "Don't even think that!"

"But those crooks don't want us around," Bert went on. "You never know what they might do."

Cherry promised to keep an eye peeled for the little girl, and Bert trotted across the bridge to the animal island. He found the zoo keeper and asked if his sister had been there.

"You mean Lulu's little friend?" the man asked with a smile.

"Yes. The blond one."

"She came about half an hour ago to visit the chimp, but Lulu isn't here."

"Did Lulu break loose again?"

"No. She had an accident. Hurt a leg, and I had to take her to the vet."

"Where did my sister go?" Bert asked.

"She walked off with two little boys. I thought perhaps they were more of your family."

"No, they don't belong to us. Well, thanks a lot. I'll keep searching."

Bert made his way back across the bridge, looking sharply for Flossie and her new friends.

There were many children, singly or in groups, walking along and chatting gaily. But no Flossie. Bert started to get nervous. He stopped at the next phone booth and dialed Number 3, but was told Flossie had not yet been found!

Bert continued toward the center of the amusement area. Now and then he stepped on a bench to look over the heads of the crowd for his sister. Then he heard music. A band was playing.

The boy knew that Flossie loved to watch parades, so he hurried to where the music was coming from.

"What's going on?" he asked a cowboy officer.

"There's an Oriental parade over on the next block. If you hurry, you can see it!"

By now other visitors had been attracted to the music and were moving toward the parade route. Bert dodged in and out among people until he found a spot along the crowded street. Several floats had already passed by.

Now came a dragon, zigzagging along. It had six legs and its fierce-looking head was breathing white smoke.

It was then that Bert saw his sister on the opposite curb. "Flossie!" he shouted.

At that moment Nan was at the control center of the World of Fun, the TV monitors before her. She was immensely relieved as she noticed Flossie sitting on the curb with two small boys, one on each side of her. The little girl clapped and waved as the dragon came closer.

Then Nan noticed Bert. He started to run across the street toward his sister, but the dragon suddenly veered in his direction and Bert was tripped by one of the six legs.

Down he went—and the dragon fell in a heap on top of him!

Nan reached for the phone to call Pete. But the continuing TV scene caused her to stop and stare with fright. Three bears were cavorting around Flossie. While the Mother Bear stopped to talk to the little girl, the Father Bear tried to pull her away.

But Flossie would not go with him and her two new friends tugged at her.

By this time Bert had freed himself. He scrambled to his feet and got hold of his sister while the Three Bears melted into the crowd.

"I'm so glad they're gone!" Nan said with a sigh of relief. "And Flossie's all right now. Bert saved her in time!"

She called the security office and reported what she had seen to Pete Prescott. Her eyes were still on the monitor even while she spoke to him.

A minute or two later she saw two cowboys

The dragon fell on top of Bert!

arrive at the scene to take charge of the three youngsters. He took them and Bert away in a chuck wagon.

"I'll go and meet them at Pete's office," Nan decided. "And I better tell them about those bears." She had noticed something that made them look different and thought this might be a good clue.

The public address system called Mr. and Mrs. Bobbsey. They arrived with Freddie at Pete's office fifteen minutes later. Nan was already there, along with a Mrs. Svenson, the mother of the two little boys who had also wandered off.

Just then the officers came in with Bert, Flossie and the boys.

"Goodness, what happened to you?" Mrs. Bobbsey cried and lifted Flossie up into her arms.

"I looked around, Mommy, and you weren't there," Flossie replied.

"You should have gone to a cowboy policeman!" her father said.

"I know that," Flossie said, wrinkling her nose. "But I thought I'd visit Lulu first because there was no cowboy around. And then I met Eric and David."

Both boys, holding tightly to their mother's hands, bobbed their heads, and Eric, who was

Freddie's age, said, "We had such a good time with Flossie!"

Mrs. Svenson thanked the Bobbsey girl for taking care of her youngsters and they left Pete's office just as a voice over the intercom announced, "Some loot has been found, Chief!"

"Where?"

"Out on the circus grounds. An ex-clown named Molo has been arrested."

"We had something to do with that," Bert spoke up, and told what had happened the night before.

"I also have some other good information for you, Pete!" Nan said.

"What's that?"

"I saw it while I watched the TV monitor. It's about the three bears who tried to capture Flossie just before Bert rescued her. Their outfits were different from other bears I've seen. You know the gold buttons down their front?"

"Yes, of course."

"These bears had four of them. All the rest have five!"

Pete Prescott thumped his desk. "Nan Bobbsey," he said, "you've supplied the answer to this mystery. I'll bet those bears don't work for the World of Fun at all! They're fakes!"

CHAPTER XI

THE SKELETON'S WARNING

PETE Prescott spoke into his intercom: "Attention, security men! Arrest all bears with only four buttons on their costumes!"

Then he turned to the Bobbseys. "I'm going to join this search, myself. We must catch these scoundrels before they can do any more mischief."

He paused, then addressed the twins' parents. "I could use some more sharp eyes. Could you lend me Bert and Nan for a while?"

"Of course," Mr. Bobbsey replied.

"Good. Come this way, kids. My chuck wagon is outside."

Bert and Nan hopped into the police car and

Pete set off along the crowded streets. He was in constant radio touch with the TV monitors at the computer room.

The Bobbseys looked right and left as Pete threaded through the tourists. No sight of the Three Bears with the four-button costumes!

Then word came over the radio. "Three Bad Bears on road leading to seaplane dock!"

Pete beeped his horn continually and picked up speed. "Oh, dear!" Nan said. "I hope they're not out to harm Cherry!"

"Do you still see them?" Pete radioed after a few minutes.

"No. They're off the screen."

"Will we get there in time to catch them?" Nan asked.

"We'd better!" Bert declared.

Now the seaplane base came into sight and as the chuck wagon zigzagged through half a dozen dancing Snow White and Seven Dwarf clowns, Nan got the first glimpse of the Bears. They were walking very fast toward the dock!

Cherry was helping a passenger into her plane. She stood by the door, looking very comical in her makeup. Suddenly the Bears ran to the aircraft and the Father Bear tried to push Cherry inside!

"They're going to hijack *The Flying Clown!*" Nan cried out.

"Not if I can help it!" Pete declared. With screeching brakes he stopped his chuck wagon near the edge of the dock, jumped out and raced up to the seaplane.

"Halt!" he cried out. "All three of you! You're under arrest!"

To Bert he said, "Get on the radio and tell my men the situation. Ask for another chuck wagon."

The Bears stopped momentarily, then began to dance around in a circle.

"I mean it!" Pete said. "You don't work for us. You're impostors!"

He walked toward the Father Bear. Just then the three of them bent low and ran at him like football players. The weight of the bears was too much for the security chief.

Pete was pushed toward the end of the dock, and while Nan and Cherry screamed in horror, he fell backward into the water!

The Bears raced to the chuck wagon where Bert had just finished giving his message.

"Get out of here, kid!" the Mother Bear growled, grabbing Bert by the arm. The boy was yanked so hard that he fell to the ground.

Then the Three Bears climbed in, turned around, and set off along the road toward the center of the amusement park.

Bert picked himself up out of the dust and

Pete fell backward into the water!

raced after the chuck wagon, with Nan at his heels. But they were soon outdistanced.

At the dock, meanwhile, Pete swam to a ladder and climbed out of the water, dripping wet.

"Are you all right?" Cherry asked, while a few startled passengers peered out the window of *The Flying Clown.*

"I'm not hurt," Pete said. "Just embarrassed and very angry. Those crooks won't give me the slip again!"

At that moment another chuck wagon, which Bert had summoned, appeared from the opposite direction. A cowboy riding in it got out and the security chief took over. He climbed behind the wheel and sent orders to all of his men to be on the alert for the three fugitives.

To the cowboy he said, "I want you to guard the dock. It seemed the crooks meant to hijack the plane and they might be back. Call me if they do!"

"Okay, Chief," the man said.

Bert and Nan returned to the dock and Pete said, "Come on. We'll catch them yet!"

The two hopped aboard and Pete drove as fast as he could, honking for pedestrians to get out of his way. But the Bears had disappeared from sight.

They proceeded for about a half mile when the Bobbseys heard music.

"It sounds like a fife-and-drum corps," Bert said.

"That's right," Pete agreed. "A Boy Scout parade was scheduled today."

When they came closer, Nan cried out, "There they are. I see them!"

"The Boy Scouts?" Bert asked.

"No, the Bears! They're in the chuck wagon trying to push through the kids!"

Pete had to chuckle when he realized what was happening. There were only about fifty scouts, but more than a hundred youngsters trailed along behind them, marching to the cadence of the drums.

"They'll never make it!" Bert said gleefully.

Pete parked the wagon. Everyone jumped out and ran toward the Bears, who were trying to inch through the wall of children.

The Mother Bear turned around and when she noticed the security chief, shouted a warning to the others.

The three dived out of the chuck wagon, split up, and made their way helter-skelter through the crowd.

"I'll go after the big one!" Pete said. "Bert, you follow the Mother Bear, and Nan, you keep your eye on the Baby."

All three went off in different directions. Bert noticed that the clown he was to follow carried a small package.

"More loot!" the boy thought to himself.

The clown was a very fast runner, and every time he broke into an open space he put more distance between himself and the Bobbsey boy.

Twice Bert saw Nan hurrying on her way, and once he heard Pete shouting for the Big Bear to stop.

It was a cat-and-mouse race, right up to the main street. Bert still had his quarry in sight and was a half block away when he saw the clown disappear into the Haunted House.

Pete and Nan raced up behind Bert just as his parents and the younger twins appeared from another direction.

"What's going on?" Mrs. Bobbsey asked, seeing Nan, Bert, and the chief flushed and winded.

"We're each chasing a Bad Bear," Bert said. "Mine just went into the Haunted House."

"We lost track of ours," Pete declared. He sounded frustrated. "But we'll catch that fellow in there!"

He asked Bert to stand by the exit, then arranged with the ticket taker to admit the Bobbseys free because they were on police duty. Quickly they filed into the dimly lighted old house.

It looked as if it had been built a hundred years ago, with ornate rooms, ancient furniture and funny old pictures on the wall.

But the strangest things were the wax dummies scattered about throughout the rooms. They appeared so lifelike that Freddie and Flossie gasped.

In the dimness Captain Kidd raised his cutlass menacingly and Freddie backed away from the figure. They entered another room, and a devil with his pitchfork glared, fire coming out of his eyes.

Suddenly there was a loud moan and heavy chains rattled. A high-pitched voice said, "I want my body!"

Several tourists uttered screams when they heard this, while others laughed.

In an even darker room a ghostly figure stepped from a closet, then disappeared through a blackened window.

Nan sucked in air audibly and even Mrs. Bobbsey said, "Goodness, that was frightening!"

Now the wind howled up a chimney, an owl hooted, and Frankenstein's monster reached out from behind a blowing curtain.

"Keep your eyes open for the bear," came Pete's voice. This seemed to break the spell that hung over the twins.

"I almost forgot about the bear," Flossie whispered to Nan.

"Me, too. This place is so spooky!"

They passed another horror scene. Deep in

a dark corner stood a skeleton. Its bones shone ghostly and its face bore a menacing grin.

Freddie was fascinated. He let go of Nan's hand while the others walked on. Intently he stared at the skeleton and suddenly called out in a small voice, "Nan, come back quick! I want to show you something!"

"Did you see the bear?" his sister asked.

"No. Something else. Hurry!"

"Oh, come on, Freddie. We're close to the exit."

"I know, but look!"

Nan came to his side. Several other sightseers bumped into them in the darkness.

"What is it, Freddie?"

"The skeleton moved!"

"That's just your imagination!" Nan said.

Suddenly she froze and stood rooted in horror. The skeleton raised its arms slowly and advanced toward them.

Nan shook loose from her fear and said, "I suppose it's a mechanical skeleton, Freddie."

But the oncoming figure did not stop. Instead, it reached out two bony hands and caught Freddie and Nan around the neck!

Its gruesome face pressed close to theirs and it hissed in a creaky voice, "Leave this place by tomorrow, or you'll all become skeletons!"

Nan's screams sounded through the Haunted House!

CHAPTER XII

THE THIRTEENTH
SLEEPYHEAD

WAITING at the exit, Bert Bobbsey heard Nan scream in terror. He jumped over the turnstile and ran inside just as all the lights went on.

People were milling about, asking one another what had happened.

"It sounds as if someone was badly hurt," a woman said. Bert pushed against the tide of visitors trying to get out until he reached his family.

Pete saw him and said, "Everything is under control now. No one's hurt. Please return to the exit, Bert. The person who frightened Nan and Freddie could slip out in all this confusion!"

Bert hastened back, scolding himself for not having stuck to his post.

The others searched through the Haunted House, but the skeleton had disappeared. Nobody was hiding in the various rooms, but near the fake window, through which the ghost had vanished, Nan saw something suspicious lying on the floor.

"Pete," she called out. "Come over here!" She bent down to pick up what seemed to be discarded clothing. "A bear suit!" she cried. "And here's the skeleton costume!"

The others rushed up and Pete examined the suits carefully. "This tells the story," he said. "Our bear came in here, changed into the skeleton outfit that was on the wax dummy, and after he frightened you, took it off and escaped!"

At the exit, Bert said he had not seen the bear and told the officer how sorry he was that he had left his post temporarily.

Pete grinned and gave him a pat on the shoulder. "Don't worry about it. The man, no doubt, wore regular clothes when he walked out, and you wouldn't have recognized him, anyway."

"I suppose you can't win 'em all," Bert said ruefully.

"No. But if my new plan works, we'll capture those rascals soon," Pete said.

The younger twins had wandered off out of earshot when Pete revealed his strategy.

"Tomorrow there will be no World of Fun

animal clowns on the streets. They'll all have the day off!"

"I get the idea!" Bert exclaimed. "If any clowns do appear, they'll be the thieves!"

"Right. And we'll pounce on them," the security chief declared.

"What an excellent plan!" Mrs. Bobbsey said. "Is there anything we can do to help you?"

"I think you've had enough excitement for one day," Pete said. "Why don't you just enjoy yourselves for the rest of the afternoon? I'll let you know if anything else develops."

"Good. I'm hungry," Nan said.

"It's past lunchtime," Mrs. Bobbsey agreed. "Where shall we eat?"

"How about another Moon Dog?" Bert suggested. "I know how to get to the space wheel. Follow me."

They called Freddie and Flossie and went to the restaurant.

After lunch Mr. Bobbsey said, "What would you like to see next?"

"The Old Lady in the Shoe!" Flossie said. "I'd like to see all her children."

Everyone agreed and on the way Bert stopped in front of a photo shop. "Dad, look at this!" he said, pointing to a camera on a piece of black velvet. "It takes instant pictures. We've always wanted one like it!"

The sign above it read: Best Bargain in the World of Fun.

Mr. Bobbsey glanced at the price tag. "It *is* a good deal," he admitted. "And it has a flash attachment, too."

"Could we buy it, please?" Nan pleaded.

"Please, pretty please?" Flossie urged.

"All right," Mr. Bobbsey agreed. "Let's go in and take a look."

Ten minutes later the Bobbseys trooped out of the shop with Bert carrying their new camera on a strap around his neck.

"What'll we take pictures of?" he asked.

Mr. Bobbsey chuckled at his son's impatience. "You'll find something, I'm sure," he said.

Freddie and Flossie skipped on ahead and waited at the entrance to the exhibit while their father bought six tickets.

"Here's where the Old Lady lives," Freddie said.

Soon all bent low as they went through a small door in the toe of the shoe.

It led to a large room dimly lighted by a candle sitting on a low table. Beside it an old-fashioned-looking woman rocked back and forth in an old-fashioned chair.

"Is—is she real?" Flossie asked.

"No, it's just a figure," her mother replied.

"Here's where the Old Lady lives," Freddie said.

As their eyes became accustomed to the dimness, the visitors saw a large bed next to the woman. On it were sprawled her children, all fast asleep.

Nan giggled and said, "Look at the funny positions they're in!"

"They must have been pretty tired when they flopped down," Bert said.

The children were sleeping head-to-toe and toe-to-head. Some were in figure S's. The twins were amazed by the lifelike appearance of the dummies.

"That little girl with the braids is so pretty!" Flossie said loudly.

"And see the boy lying on his face? His blond hair looks just like yours," Nan said.

Bert had walked up a narrow ramp behind the bed and focused the camera. A flash of light pierced the darkness.

"Bert took a picture!" Freddie said. "Come on, let's see how it came out."

The children hurried to the exit at the heel of the shoe and Bert had the picture developed just as they stepped back into the street. The family crowded around to look at it.

"That's great!" Mrs. Bobbsey said. "How many kids are there? Let's see."

Nan quickly counted. "Thirteen."

"A baker's dozen!" Mr. Bobbsey smiled.

An attendant, standing near the exit, heard this. "Thirteen?" he asked. "Did you say the old woman has thirteen children?"

"That's right," Bert said.

"Sorry. There are only twelve figures in that bed," the attendant told him.

Nan showed him the photograph. He studied it, then said, "One of them doesn't belong here. I'll take a look myself."

"Maybe the extra one is Howie!" Nan said. "Now we can catch him."

Their father bought another six tickets and they quickly followed the attendant inside. Everyone counted the children lying on the big bed. There were only twelve!

"The boy with the blond hair who was lying on his face is gone!" Nan cried out. "Now I'm sure it was Howie!"

"Maybe the girls' giggling awakened him," Bert said.

"Or he might have seen you take the picture," Nan said.

"Oh, dear," Flossie said. "We're not very good at catching people, are we?"

Outside again, Mrs. Bobbsey said, "I think we better see Cherry and tell her about Howie."

"I'm getting tired," Flossie complained, and her father hoisted her to his broad shoulders.

"All right," he said. "I'll give you a ride to the seaplane dock."

They arrived at the dock just in time to see Cherry land the pontoon plane gently on the lagoon. She taxied up to the dock, and the passengers got out, thanking her for the pleasant flight.

Flossie wriggled down from her father's shoulders and ran up to her. "We saw him! We saw Howie in the old woman's bed!"

"What?"

Nan told the puzzled girl what had happened.

Cherry shook her head. "Well, at least he's getting his sleep."

Since it had been the *Flying Clown's* last trip for the day, she walked back with the Bobbseys to where the performers applied their makeup. On the way they talked of the mystery.

"I was thinking about what that angry man said to Molo," Cherry said, "about the big job and the island. It may be along the coast here somewhere."

"Could we see it from your airplane?" Bert asked.

"I suppose we could if we knew where to look," Cherry replied. "Why don't we try it tomorrow afternoon? I'll take you all up after my scheduled flights."

"That would be great!" Flossie said.

"Come to the dock at four," Cherry suggested.

"We'll be there!" Flossie and Nan hugged her and the Bobbseys started back toward the African Village.

They went in the pool for a refreshing swim and at supper the hungry twins shared an extra order of French fries.

"Who's awake enough to see the fireworks?" Mr. Bobbsey asked. "It's Friday and there will be displays tonight and tomorrow."

"I am!" all four children chorused eagerly.

The show was to last twenty minutes, ending with a bombardment of flying stars.

Everyone found comfortable seats around the pool when the rockets started to hiss up out of the volcano. There were "Oh's" and "Ah's" at the colorful display.

Suddenly everything stopped.

"It only lasted about three minutes!" Freddie complained.

"I'm disappointed, too," Nan said.

Then an announcement came over the motel speaker system. "There will be no more fireworks tonight. The park management will try to renew the entertainment tomorrow evening."

"Something must have gone wrong," Bert said, rising from his lounge chair. "I'm going to call Pete and find out what happened."

He hurried into his bedroom and dialed the

number. Pete was not there, but the officer in charge spoke to him. When he had finished, Bert thanked him and ran out to the poolside.

"Guess what!" he called out. "A whole load of fireworks has been stolen!"

"I wonder how those mean thieves managed that," Nan said.

"Maybe it was the big haul they were talking about," Mrs. Bobbsey suggested. "Fireworks are very expensive."

"They might have taken the stuff out through the underground," Bert reasoned. "And we haven't even seen that place yet."

The weary family went off to their huts and Freddie flopped down on his bed. Even before Bert could get into his pajamas, Freddie was sound asleep.

Bert took off his brother's clothes and put pajamas on him. Freddie slept through it all.

Next morning everyone was up early, eager for new adventures. After breakfast, the boys wandered to the back of the grounds and peered over the fence where the ugly intruder had disappeared the first night. The area resembled dense jungle, with palmettos, pines, and palm trees.

They went back to the motel and asked Mrs. Mingo what was behind it.

"The Jungle Railroad," she replied. "I recommend you take a ride on it. You'll see how Indians lived—and still do—in their chickees."

"What's that?" Freddie asked.

Mrs. Mingo explained that a chickee was a thatched roof shelter supported by poles and having no side walls.

"Let's go see the chickens right now!" Freddie said impatiently.

"We'll have to ask Mom or Dad first," Bert said.

In their parents' hut, Mrs. Bobbsey was giving the girls shampoos.

"May Freddie and I ride on the Jungle Railroad?" Bert asked.

"Certainly. Go ahead. I want to take the girls shopping, as soon as their hair is dry."

Mr. Bobbsey gave Bert some money and the boys ran off to find the entrance. It turned out to be quite a distance away, and as they approached the place, they could hear the *chug-chug-chug* of a steam engine.

A miniature locomotive pulled six open railway cars. Bert and Freddie climbed in and found two seats way in the back. With a slight jerk and a long whistle blast the train started off on its narrow tracks.

They went over swamps where real alligators swam about, then onto higher ground past three Indian chickees which were grouped about a dead campfire. Scantily clad figures with small children looked as lifelike as the spooks in the Haunted House.

Farther on they passed a scene which showed turtle poachers wrestling with a giant sea turtle.

"I hope it gets away," Freddie said.

Now a small stream came into view with three Indian dugouts pulled halfway up on the bank.

"This jungle is getting wilder and wilder," Bert remarked, his eyes fixed on another settlement of chickees. Suddenly he saw a head pop up from the grass.

"Look, Freddie!" Bert whispered, excitement in his voice. "It's Howie! This time we're going to get him!"

CHAPTER XIII

THE DUCK DANCE

THE boy's head disappeared again. Bert pulled Freddie from his seat.

"Come on, we're going to jump out at the next bend!"

"Are you sure it was Howie?"

"Positive."

The train slowed and the two boys jumped off. They rolled over a couple of times in the soft grass and finally stopped in a sitting position.

The jungle train disappeared in the distance.

"Are you okay?" Bert asked Freddie.

"Yes. Now what?"

"Follow me on your hands and knees."

Like jungle cats, they slithered through the grass until they reached the spot where Howie's head had popped up. It was right next to a chickee.

Bert raised himself for a better view. There was Howie, inside the hut, moving to the far end!

Bert and Freddie jumped up and raced toward the runaway.

Startled by the sudden appearance of the Bobbseys, the boy hesitated for a moment. This gave Bert time to leap upon him. Down they went in a heap!

Freddie grabbed Howie by the feet and Bert sat on his chest.

"All right, you've got me," the captured boy said. "Let me up now."

"Not till you promise that you won't run away!" Bert said. He looked down into the freckled face and could see that Howie was not pleased. But the boy mumbled, "I promise."

When the Bobbseys let him up, he said, "I think I know where the thieves are hiding out."

"Why don't you tell security?" Bert asked.

"I will. And then I'll confess."

"Confess what?" Freddie asked.

"I did something bad," Howie continued.

"What?" Bert inquired.

"I can't tell now."

Bert decided not to press Howie and changed the subject. "How did you know we were coming to Florida?"

"I went into the motel lobby to get a drink of water," Howie replied. "And I overheard the lady telling about the detective family from Lakeport who was coming to visit."

"That must have been Mrs. Mingo!"

Howie nodded.

"But if you want us to help you, why did you run away from us all the time?"

"Because the gang's forever after me. And they're watching you, too. It became too dangerous for me to contact you."

The boy ran a finger through his blond hair. "Look here, I found a secret entrance!"

He pulled a straw mat from the floor of the chickee. Underneath was a trapdoor. It had a ring to pull it open. The words "Emergency Exit" were written under it.

"I discovered this while I was exploring the underground," Howie said. "Probably not many people know about this."

He took a flashlight from his pocket and aimed a light beam down onto a narrow metal stairway. Then he started to descend.

"You want to come with me?"

"Where are you going?" Bert asked.

"To the hideout."

"Okay, we'll help."

"Pull the door in place quietly," Howie warned, as Freddie and Bert climbed down the stairs after him.

Under the chickee the air was stuffy and smelled like cement.

"I've been here lots of times," Howie said in a low voice as they crawled through a narrow passage lined with pipes. "Some of these pipes are very hot, so you've got to be careful."

Just then Freddie touched one and cried out.

"Sh-sh!" Howie warned. "Don't do that, or you'll give us away!"

Freddie put his burned finger into his mouth and sucked on it. They continued on, stooping low to avoid the obstructions. Finally the passage opened into a wide corridor with doors on either side.

"This is where a lot of the World of Fun stuff is kept," Howie whispered. He flashed his light to the end of the corridor where the passage turned right.

"I think the thieves are hiding in a room around the corner," he said. "From now on we must be extra quiet."

The boys tiptoed along. They made the turn, and twenty feet later Howie directed his light at one of the doors. It bore the words "Miscellaneous Storage."

"What does that mean?" Freddie asked.

"Odds and ends," Bert replied. "Now hush up."

Howie pressed his ear to the door and Bert did the same. Somebody was inside, but all they could hear was mumbling. Howie turned the doorknob gently. They all held their breaths as he pushed the heavy door open a crack.

Now they could hear the conversation very well. Three men were talking.

"I say we've got to lay low a day or two until we get new outfits," one of them said. Bert recognized the voice. It was the man who had been scolding Molo at the circus trailer!

With a chuckle the fellow added, "Blinky, you really scared the wits out of those Bobbsey kids."

"Yeah, boss. That was funny!"

A third voice said, "I'll bet my share of the loot that the Bobbseys will clear out of here by morning."

"Good," the first fellow declared. "That'll give us a couple of days to plan for the big job. We'll make it perfect."

"But wait a minute, boss," Blinky said. "There's one thing we ought to do right away."

"What's that?"

"Get Howie. I saw him hanging around the chickee. He might have learned about the emer-

MISCELLANEOUS
STORAGE

Howie turned the doorknob gently.

gency exit and could really blow the whistle on us."

"Right. But the kid's afraid of the cops since he swiped those disguises."

So that was it! Howie's secret was out.

"I took that old man's suit and the Ugly Duckling costume so I could spy on them without being recognized," Howie whispered. "The first one I returned, but not the other one, because the place was locked up."

"Don't worry," Bert whispered back.

The voice of the gang leader sounded again. "We'll fan out tonight and catch Howie. I heard one of the cowboys say that a kid was sleeping with the children of the Old Woman in the Shoe."

"Pretty clever," Blinky said. "Tomorrow he'll be sleeping on the island."

"Is the boat ready, Spinner?" the boss asked.

"Rearing to go. All tuned up for our getaway after the big job."

Howie tiptoed away from the door and motioned to Bert. Then he said, "I'm going to stay here and listen some more. Maybe they'll mention where the island is. You get to a phone and notify Mr. Prescott about their hiding place. Take my flashlight. I know my way in the dark."

"Okay."

"And listen. I hid the Ugly Duckling costume behind your hut in some bushes. Take it and give it to Mr. Prescott, too. I'll turn myself in this afternoon."

Bert and Freddie made their way cautiously through the maze of pipes while Howie went back to listen at the door.

Finally they came to the iron stairway. Bert climbed up ahead and opened the trapdoor. He and Freddie stepped out into the jungle chickee. They were about to replace the cover when they heard a fearful commotion going through the underground tunnel.

The boss's voice bellowed furiously, "It's the kid. Get him, Blinky!"

There was an outcry, then all was silent again.

"They've captured Howie!" Freddie exclaimed. "Bert, we've got to help him!"

Meanwhile, Flossie Bobbsey skipped into the African Village. Her freshly shampooed hair glistened in the Florida sunlight, and her face bore a happy expression.

Flossie found her father at the golf putting green beside the pool. "Daddy, I got a bee-yoo-ti-ful new dress!" she called out.

"Good. And where are Mother and Nan?"

"They're still looking. Nan hasn't made up her mind yet."

Mr. Bobbsey chuckled and the ball he had hit rolled *plunk!* right into the hole.

"Daddy, you're good!" Flossie giggled. "Maybe next time you'll beat Mother."

They both laughed. Then Flossie said, "Where are the boys?"

"I don't think they've returned from their jungle trip yet. But you could take a look in their hut."

Flossie skipped off and went into her brothers' quarters. They were not in. To amuse herself until they returned, she decided to investigate the grounds. She wandered behind the boys' hut into the dense shrubbery.

Suddenly she spied something yellow behind a tree.

"Maybe it's a big golden cat," the little girl thought, and went closer to pick it up.

"An Ugly Duckling suit!" Flossie stood stunned for a moment. Then she shook out the costume and inspected it curiously. An idea flashed through her head.

"This'll be fun," she told herself. "Everyone will be so surprised!"

She took the suit into her hut and wriggled into it. It was far too big for her. But she zipped up the front, dropped the hood over her face, and walked in front of the mirror.

"Quack, quack, quack!" she said, waving her

wings. She waddled toward the door, nearly tripping over her duck feet.

"Mother and Nan should be coming back soon," Flossie thought. "I'll go out and meet them."

When she reached the street, a crowd of people gathered around her and laughed. "That certainly is a comical duck," one woman said. "Here, Ugly Duckling, I want to take your picture."

Two cowboy officers noticed all the people and while Flossie was having a good time doing a duck dance, they pushed through the tourists.

"Here's one of them!" the older cowboy called out and grabbed Flossie by the arm.

The other one spoke into his walkie-talkie. "This is Jones calling headquarters. We've just found an animal clown. An Ugly Duckling. Your plan worked! This one's so small, my guess is he's a circus midget!"

Then he turned to Flossie and said in a stern voice, "No more funny games for you! You're under arrest!"

CHAPTER XIV

THREE MEN IN THE BOAT

BACK at the jungle railroad, Bert and Freddie ran along the narrow tracks. They hoped the next train would come so they could report the location of the thieves' hideout and the capture of poor Howie.

"If we don't get word to Pete Prescott right away," said Bert as he jogged, "those men might escape!"

In the distance the whistle of the jungle train sounded mournful across the flat land.

"Here it comes," Bert said.

Both boys waved their arms wildly as the huffing steam engine arrived around a bend. There was a screeching of brakes. The train halted and the engineer jumped down to the side of the tracks.

"What's going on here?" he asked. "Are you in trouble?"

"We're not, but Howie is. We have to get to a telephone as soon as possible."

"And tell Pete Prescott all about it," Freddie added.

"Well, hop on. You can call from the next stop, Number 5."

The boys climbed aboard, with the other passengers looking at them curiously.

In a few minutes the jungle station came into view. Bert stepped off the train, with Freddie close behind him. They hastened to a phone booth and dialed number 3.

The operator put Bert through to the security chief. "Pete? This is Bert Bobbsey. I'm calling from Jungle Stop Number 5. Howie and Freddie and I found out where the crooks are hiding!"

Bert told about the storage room and Pete said, "Good. Stay right where you are. And don't let Howie get away this time."

"But the thieves caught him!"

"What? I'll be right over with my men."

The chief and two cowboys arrived on an empty train in a few minutes. They picked up the Bobbseys, then backed up to the chickee.

"Other men are approaching the storeroom through the underground," Pete said, hurrying to the stairway where he had left two cowboys to guard the exit.

When Pete and the boys reached the storeroom, all they found were the other police who had arrived just before them. No thieves were in sight, and neither was Howie!

"They got away!" Pete fumed. "Probably through the chickee."

They returned to the hidden exit and spread out, looking for any trail the thieves might have left.

"Here's where they went!" one of the officers called out. He pointed to flattened grass. It left a distinct path right up to the stream, where the boys had seen the three dugouts from the train. Only two were left!

"They must have paddled away," Bert said, disappointed.

"Where does this little river go?" Freddie asked.

"Into the lagoon," Pete replied and spoke into his walkie-talkie. "Check the lagoon for three men and a boy in a dugout. The men are dangerous. In case of resistance, don't let any harm come to the youngster."

Then Pete, Bert, and Freddie took one of the dugouts. Two other officers followed in the second craft.

"This is fun!" Freddie said excitedly. He sat in the middle, while Pete in back and Bert in front paddled furiously along the winding waterway.

"It couldn't have been much fun for Howie," Bert said, and Freddie remained silent for the next ten minutes until they reached the lagoon.

They looked about, but neither the men nor the kidnapped boy could be seen. A few minutes later they found an abandoned canoe near the place where the lagoon entered the open water. The two officers checked it out, while Pete and the boys questioned several passing boatmen.

No one had seen the fugitives. But when the two policemen pulled alongside, one of them said, "This is what we found in the dugout." He handed the chief an old glass marble.

"Howie was in that boat for sure!" Bert exclaimed. "Cherry told us about his antique marble collection."

"Then we're on the right trail," Pete said.

They interviewed more boatmen, to no avail. Finally Bert saw a boy pumpimg a pedal boat near the entrance to the lagoon. He cupped his hands and called out their question. The boy stopped.

"Yes, I saw three men and a kid in a motorboat," the boy yelled back. "Their waves almost made me tip over!"

"Which way did they go?"

The boy gestured toward open water.

"Was it a big boat?"

"About fifteen feet. With two outboard motors. Very powerful—named *Circus Princess*."

"Thanks!"

Pete talked into his radio again, this time alerting police along the coast to be on the lookout for *Circus Princess*. He also asked to have a wagon ready for him at the seaplane dock.

Then, as they paddled to shore, Bert said, "Now we know how these thieves got the loot out of the World of Fun—by boat! They hid the stuff in that storeroom, carried it out to the chickee, and floated it along the stream and out into the lagoon here. Then they picked it up with their speedboat."

"Well, we can plug up that leak," said Freddie in a manly voice.

Pete smiled and the Indian canoes were beached near where Cherry berthed her plane.

The wagon Pete had ordered was already there, and everyone climbed aboard. Just as they were ready to leave, his walkie-talkie squawked.

"Headquarters calling Pete Prescott. Urgent message."

"Here I am, go ahead."

"Jones has spotted an animal clown."

"What kind? Bear?"

"No. A small Ugly Duckling. Near the African Village."

"I'm on my way," Pete said, and clicked off.

"That's not too far from here," Bert said. "We live there."

Pete bent over the wheel and drove as fast as he could. The street near the Bobbseys' motel was full of curious onlookers. Pete parked the cart and they all pushed through the crowd.

When they reached the center of the commotion, the two boys were surprised to see their mother and two sisters. Mrs. Bobbsey was holding Flossie in her arms. A cowboy officer stood next to them examining an Ugly Duckling suit.

"There, there, now," Mrs. Bobbsey said. "No one's going to arrest you, dear."

Flossie's shoulders shook with a few more sobs. Then, looking through her tears, she saw Pete and smiled.

"What's going on here?" the security chief asked.

When the whole story came to light, everyone chuckled.

"We should have told Freddie and Flossie about our plan to catch the Bad Bears," Pete said. "You'll have to forgive us, little lady."

One of the cowboys had walked off and now returned with a double-scoop ice cream cone,

"No one's going to arrest you, dear."

which he handed to Flossie. "Now, don't get salty tears on the vanilla," he said, smiling.

Mrs. Bobbsey took out a handkerchief and wiped the little girl's cheeks as she thanked the officers.

Pete then told the family that he would be in close touch and said good-by for the moment. The Bobbseys went back into the African Village and found Mr. Bobbsey sitting in the shade of a palm tree.

"Wait till you hear what happened to us!" Bert said.

The adventures were quickly recounted and their father was amazed to hear all that had taken place.

"And here I was, relaxing in the sun, missing all the action," he said ruefully.

"That's all right," Flossie said, nibbling on her ice cream cone. "You can play detective with us for the rest of the day. You're coming along in the *Flying Clown,* aren't you?"

"Of course."

"That reminds me," Nan said. "I should call Cherry and tell her about Howie."

Nan reached the pilot and Mrs. Bobbsey spoke to her, too. "I'm sure your brother will be found," she assured the worried girl. "Everybody is working on the case."

Cherry was very disturbed, but then got hold

of herself. "I'll expect you here at four o'clock," she said. "Anyway, now we know what to look for, the *Circus Princess.* I have several pairs of binoculars aboard. They'll probably come in handy."

At a quarter of four they were at the dock, and Cherry came up to meet them. She was wearing her clown's makeup, but beneath it her expression was one of deep anxiety.

Nan hugged her and said, "Don't worry, Cherry, Howie'll be all right."

"I don't know. It's worse than I thought." The girl sighed.

"What do you mean?"

"I just got a note from the kidnappers."

"What?"

Cherry pulled a piece of paper from her pocket. On it was a message printed in pencil. It said, "If you want to see Howie alive again, leave the *Flying Clown* unlocked and ready for takeoff at 8:00 P.M., Monday night. Don't tell the police!"

CHAPTER XV

A BIG MISTAKE

THE Bobbseys were shocked by the kidnappers' note.

"Oh, that's terrible!" Mrs. Bobbsey said. "You will tell the police, won't you, Cherry?"

"Of course I will," the girl replied. "But that can wait until we return from our flight. We may have some extra information to give them."

As they all got into the seaplane, Bert and Nan were busy trying to figure out what the kidnappers had in mind.

"Obviously, they want a getaway plane," Bert said. "That brings up two possibilities." He reasoned that one of the thieves must be a pilot. "Also, it means that their big job will take place right here at the World of Fun."

Cherry cast off the rope holding the plane to the dock, and started the engine. The propeller sparkled golden in the late afternoon sun, pulling the *Flying Clown* over the water in the lagoon.

While the Bobbseys watched, fascinated, Cherry revved it up and pulled back on the wheel. The pontoons bounced over the wavelets and the plane was airborne.

Cherry circled out over the sea, then flew north along the coast.

Nan moved up into the seat beside her. "I don't know how we're going to find the *Circus Princess*," she said. "Just look at all the traffic down there!"

Far below, the speedboats seemed like tiny bugs trailing frothy plumes over the sparkling sea.

Once Cherry was far enough away from the amusement center, she brought the plane lower over the waves. Then she told Nan to open a compartment at the side of her seat. In it were two pairs of binoculars.

"You and Bert can use these!" she said.

Nan handed one pair to her brother, and together they scanned the speedy motorboats.

After ten minutes of fruitless searching, the older twins gave the glasses to Freddie and Flossie. Another ten minutes passed, then the children's arms grew weary.

"Here, Mommy and Daddy, you look for a while," Flossie said.

Their parents took the binoculars and while Cherry whizzed over a group of small islands, they surveyed the water below.

"Finding a needle in a haystack," Mrs. Bobbsey said, "would be easier than this!"

"It looks like everybody in Florida owns a boat!" Mr. Bobbsey declared.

After they had been up in the air for an hour, Cherry said, "I'll have to go back now. We're getting low on fuel."

She banked the *Flying Clown* gracefully over the sea, and, still flying low, returned toward the World of Fun.

Halfway to home base, Nan saw the long trailing wake of a speedboat. "That one's traveling awfully fast," she said to herself as she trained the binoculars on its stern. She could not make out the name, but saw that there were three men in it.

"Cherry, could you come a little closer for that one?" she asked, pointing out the craft.

The plane turned, at the same time dropping lower. Now Nan noticed a large sack on the floor of the boat. The lettering was still indistinct, however.

She called to her father, "Daddy, can you read the name with the other binoculars?"

"Yes. It's something-*Princess!*"

Cherry passed over the craft. Instead of looking up, the three men seemed to hide their faces.

The pilot made another pass over the boat. This time Nan got a better look at the name.

"It must be smudged with oil," she cried out. "But the first name begins with C and ends with S!"

"How many letters?" Cherry asked.

"I think six!" Nan cried. "We've discovered the *Circus Princess!*"

The Bobbseys looked on excitedly as Cherry radioed to Pete Prescott. "It seems we found our quarry, Pete," she told him, and gave the bearing.

"I'll notify the Coast Guard. Stay with them!" came the reply.

Cherry glanced at the fuel gauge. "If they get here in twenty minutes, we'll be able to wait. Otherwise, I'll have to go back to the dock. I'm low on gas."

She continued flying over the boat that now was heading for a group of islands.

Suddenly it turned toward the coast. A few minutes later it reversed its course northward again.

"They're trying to get rid of us!" Bert called out. Then it hit him like a bombshell. What was in the sack at the bottom of the craft? Could it be Howie? It was large enough!

"We've discovered the *Circus Princess!*"

He whispered the thought to his mother. She nodded, and in a low voice replied, "I didn't want to alarm Cherry."

On their next pass, Bert noticed that the sack moved a little. He was convinced Howie Norton was inside!"

"I hope the Coast Guard comes soon," Cherry said. "I can't keep this up much longer!"

Just then her radio squawked a message. A Coast Guard boat was in the vicinity and had already spotted the *Flying Clown.*

"We're heading for the boat under surveillance," a guardsman informed her.

"Here they are!" Cherry said moments later as the craft came into sight.

She waggled her wings. The gas tank was nearly empty, and she glided down onto the water for a landing.

The Bobbsey twins watched in awe as the Coast Guard pulled up beside the speedboat. Cherry taxied over, and when they had come close enough, Bert opened the door and threw a line to one of the officers.

They heard an argument going on. Loud words flew back and forth. The occupants of the boat were very angry.

"What do you mean?" the skipper said. "We're peaceful citizens. You have no right to stop us!"

To Bert, the voice did not sound at all like any he had heard in the storeroom hideaway. The speaker had a squat, pug-nosed face, deeply tanned by the sun.

"This craft is the *Circus Princess*," the officer said. "You'll have to account for ownership!"

"*Circus Princess?*" the man asked in surprise. "You've got us all wrong."

One of his companions started to laugh. "I know the name on our bow is a little dirty," he said. "But it's *Cindy's Princess!*"

The third fellow said that they had been out fishing. He pointed to several rods and the sack. "We have some big ones in here, pretty lively, too," he said. "Want to see?" He opened the sack and spilled out a number of large fish. A few were still flopping.

"On the way back we tried out our new engines," he went on. "Then that plane came along and buzzed us. And now you treat us like criminals. I'd like an explanation!"

The Bobbseys felt very much embarrassed and Freddie and Flossie slid down low in their seats so as not to be seen.

"I guess that'll teach us not to jump to conclusions," Bert said, while Cherry explained their mission to the three men and apologized.

"Oh, that's all right," the skipper said. "We all make mistakes."

He asked if there was any way they could help.

"Yes, indeed," Cherry replied. "Do you have some extra gas? I'm all out."

"Sure, we can spare a couple of gallons," the man said, and the Coast Guard came up with a few more. The fuel was speedily transferred into the seaplane and the Coast Guard officer cast off the rope.

"Good luck!" he called out with a smart salute.

Cherry taxied off over the water. With the engine buzzing like a bumblebee, the *Flying Clown* rose into the sky.

Not long afterward it made a feather-like landing in the lagoon. Pete Prescott was there waiting for them.

"Got yourself in a little trouble, eh?" he said with a grin.

"I know," Cherry said. "And here we thought we'd made the big catch! But there's bigger trouble. Look at this!" She showed him the kidnappers' note.

Pete frowned and said slowly, "We'll have to think hard what to do about that." Then he winked at Flossie. "No more animal clowns showed up today!"

Flossie giggled and Bert said, "I don't think they'll ever come back."

Nan agreed. "The thieves probably will make their big haul, whatever it is, and take off in the *Flying Clown* for good."

"But what about Howie?" Cherry said nervously. "If we could only find their island hideout, we could rescue him!"

Mrs. Bobbsey spoke up. "Remember that bad chap, Horsey Raines? Has he returned to the circus yet?"

"That's a good question, Mother," Nan said. "It wouldn't hurt to check with the circus again."

"Cherry, could we drive there tonight?" Bert asked.

"Oh, dear. It'll be very late. But if your parents approve, I'll take you. Besides, I'd like to see how Old Man River is coming along."

The six-year-olds begged to go, too. "I want to see the old river man," Flossie said, stifling a big yawn.

"I'm afraid not," Mrs. Bobbsey said. "You're far too sleepy. But I'll tell you what. I'll read you two chapters of *Charlotte's Web* before bedtime."

"Oh, goody!" Flossie said. "I love spiders!"

After supper, Cherry, Bert and Nan set off once more for the circus grounds.

It was dusk when they arrived. The circus people were bustling around, dismantling the big top, and caged animals were being pulled to the nearby railroad siding.

"They're leaving tomorrow!" Cherry exclaimed. "I forgot all about it. Lucky we got here on time."

Just then a girl of eighteen passed by and noticed the *Flying Clown.*

"Are you coming back to join us?" she asked.

"Not right now," Cherry replied with a smile, and added, "Lilo, I'd like you to meet my friends Bert and Nan Bobbsey." To the twins she said, "Lilo is one of the Great Zilenkos, the high-wire performers."

"Too bad you didn't drop by earlier," Lilo said. "Then your friends could have seen some of the acts."

"I know," Cherry replied. "But we couldn't make it in time. Actually, we came to ask about Mr. Rivero. How is he?"

"He's coming along fine, but he's still in the hospital trailer."

"Do you suppose we could see him?"

"Oh, yes. You know where it is, Cherry." The girl waved and walked off.

On the way to the hospital trailer, Cherry and the Bobbseys passed Horsey Raines' quarters and saw a light in the window.

"He must be back!" Nan said excitedly.

"We'll find out after we visit Old Man River," Cherry said.

But Bert could not keep his eyes off the window. What would they do, what would they say when they met the man who had fallen into the pool? And what would he say—that is, if he was really the same person who had chased Howie?

Bert saw the curtain move slightly. Somebody looked out, then ducked down. A chill of apprehension tickled the boy's spine.

"Horsey's there, all right," he whispered to Nan.

A few minutes later Cherry knocked on the infirmary door.

"Come in," Mr. Rivero called. He wore a bathrobe and was sitting in a rocking chair.

"Hello, Mr. Rivero," Cherry said. "Do you remember Bert and Nan Bobbsey?"

The old man nodded, and in a quavering voice said, "Cherry, I'm so glad you came. We're going soon, and I feared I might never see you again."

As Cherry and the twins sat down, he went on. "There's something I must tell you before the circus moves on."

"And what is that?" Cherry asked kindly.

"I want to tell you—" the old man swallowed hard. "I want to tell you why I tried to prevent you from becoming an aerial clown!"

CHAPTER XVI

BOOM! BOOM! BOOM!

"I ALWAYS wondered why you did," Cherry said quietly.

"I know you think I've been mean," Mr. Rivero said. "I'm sorry—very sorry."

The girl reached forward and touched his bony hand. "Don't be too hard on yourself," she said. "Everything is all right now."

The clown cleared his throat. "No. Everything isn't all right. But I hope you'll forgive me when you hear what I have to say."

The Bobbseys sat spellbound, wondering what kind of confession was about to come from the circus man.

"Did you know," Old Man River went on,

his voice quavering, "that I once had a daughter?"

"No!" Cherry replied.

"Her name was Rosebud," Mr. Rivero continued. "She was beautiful, like you, Cherry. She also was an aerial clown!"

"You say she *was*—" Cherry said.

"Yes. Until the accident." Old Man River wiped at a tear. "A cable broke."

"Oh, I'm so sorry," Cherry said. "You poor man. But why didn't you tell me this before?"

"Because it was all my fault! I was the one who talked her into becoming an aerial clown. She really wanted to work with horses, but there was an opening for a high-wire girl and I pushed her into it. When I saw you wanting to do the same thing, I tried to stop you. You reminded me so much of Rosebud!"

The trailer was strangely silent for a moment. Mr. Rivero pulled out a handkerchief and blew his nose.

"So you see, Cherry, I didn't want you to be a girl clown like her."

Nan felt her eyes grow hot with tears. She saw that Old Man River's story had the same effect upon Cherry.

"Then you did it to protect me," Cherry said.

"Yes. But it was wrong. I shouldn't have tried to turn you away from the career you chose."

"That's not really why I left the circus school," Cherry said.

"Yes, I know," Mr. Rivero said. "That's another reason I'm so ashamed. I should have spoken up when Horsey played that mean trick on you."

Old Man River paused for a moment. "Cherry, we all want you back in clown school when the circus returns next year."

"I'm sure Horsey Raines doesn't," Cherry said.

"I hear he's leaving the circus soon," Old Man River said. "He hasn't been around here in quite a while."

"But we saw a light in his trailer," Nan spoke up.

"That's a friend of his. I understand he came to pick up mail and a few things for him."

The Bobbseys and Cherry said good-by to the old clown. Cherry kissed him on the cheek, and the twins shook hands.

Outside, Cherry said, "Well, that clears up part of the mystery. That poor man! He kept his heartbreak inside for such a long time!"

Bert nodded. "And now you know for sure Horsey was the one who framed you."

Cherry nodded. "Maybe we can find out some more about him from his friend. Let's go over to his trailer."

Bert knocked on Horsey's door. No one answered. The window was covered and it seemed dark inside.

"He's not here," Nan said, disappointed. "Maybe he stepped out."

"Let's look around for a while and come back later," Cherry said.

They walked away from the trailer, and Cherry said, "Let me show you how they put the animal cages on the train."

She led them to the edge of the circus grounds where railroad cars were being loaded with elephants, tigers, zebras, Wild West horses and smaller animals. Four spotlights on high poles made the area bright as day.

The circus people worked swiftly. While the Bobbseys watched, several of the animal cars were loaded and pushed off to one side into the shadows.

Suddenly someone cried out, "Tiger loose!"

Bert and Nan looked about wildly. Then they noticed the big cat. It crept out from between two cages on a flatcar and headed directly toward them!

Nan screamed and ran in one direction, Bert in another. Cherry did not move. She stood perfectly still while two men, carrying a large net, walked up behind her quietly.

One of them had a whip and cracked it at the

The tiger headed directly toward them!

crouching animal. The big tiger backed off. As it turned to run, the net was hurtled through the air. It landed squarely on the beast, who rolled over, pawing and snarling.

Pale with fright, Nan hurried back to Cherry. "You were awfully brave to stand still," she said. Then she looked about. "Where's Bert?"

"I don't know," Cherry replied, her voice shaking. "But he can't be very far."

The girls watched the circus people carry the tangled-up tiger back to his cage. They followed behind, all the time glancing around for Bert.

When the girls reached the cage, the tiger keeper said, "Look, the lock is open! Somebody did this deliberately!"

"Who would do a thing like that?" a roustabout asked angrily. "Old Raja here could have killed somebody."

"Some crazy person, no doubt," the keeper said.

It took six men to lift the tiger up. They were just about to put him into the cage, when Cherry screamed, "Stop, stop! Someone's inside!"

Two men leaped onto the flatbed car and looked into the cage. Someone in blue jeans lay bound and gagged in a corner.

The men pulled at the legs. "It's a boy!" one of them exclaimed.

"Bert!" Nan screamed.

The men released the captive and set him on the ground. Then the tiger was returned to the cage and the lock snapped shut.

"Bert, what happened?" Cherry cried, almost hysterically.

"I—I hardly know," Bert replied. "Two people grabbed me from behind. I didn't see their faces."

"Did you recognize their voices?" Nan asked.

"They didn't speak. While the tiger was being caught, they tied me up and threw me into the cage!"

"This is terrible!" Cherry said. "Somebody call the police!"

"We already did," one of the men said.

"Thanks for crying out the warning, Cherry," Bert said. "It probably saved my life!"

A few minutes later two officers appeared and interviewed everyone who had been near the cage.

"This is a serious matter," one of the policemen said. "We'll have to question the whole staff."

"May I take the children home?" Cherry asked. "It's so late already."

"Sure. Just leave the address where we can get in touch with you, if necessary."

"Before we go, I want to talk to Horsey Raines's friend," Nan declared.

"So do I," Cherry said.

The three went back to the man's trailer. It was still dark and the door was locked.

"I think he ducked out on purpose," Bert said. "He must have seen us passing by on the way to Old Man River."

"And maybe he was one of the men who grabbed you," Nan said.

"If he was," Cherry said, "he's probably far from here by now."

On the way back the three discussed the various aspects of the mystery.

"What do you think the crooks mean by their big job, Cherry?"

"High-priced jewelry, I would say," she replied. "Something easy to carry, if they hope to get away in the airplane."

Far in the distance the fireworks of the World of Fun brightened the black sky. The Bobbseys enjoyed the display. *Boom! Boom! Boom!*—the last salute sounded and the sky was dark once more.

Then another light flashed north of the World of Fun, followed by rockets shooting into the sky. A new set of fireworks, similar to that from the volcano, went off in rapid succession!

The children watched in amazement. Then Bert asked, "Cherry, is there an amusement park up that way?"

"Not that I know of," the girl replied. "Maybe it's a private celebration."

"I doubt it," Nan said. "Fireworks are expensive—and look at all the stuff that's going off! Who could afford a thing like this?"

"And why would anyone set them off so fast?" Bert said.

They continued on for a while. Bert's brain was whirling. "What's up the coast in that direction?" he asked Cherry.

"Nothing much, really. A few orange groves and several small islands off the shore."

"I've got it!" Nan cried out suddenly. "I think I have the answer!"

"What is it?" Bert asked.

"The stolen fireworks! Maybe the thieves hid them somewhere on an island and they were set off by accident. If we can find out where, we can catch those crooks and rescue Howie!"

CHAPTER XVII

STUCK!

NEXT morning Pete Prescott listened to Bert and Nan with one eyebrow raised. He doubted their theory that the stolen fireworks had blown up accidentally.

"Young people have been known to shoot off sky rockets on those islands," he said. "They go out in motorboats for evening beach parties. You'll find burned out bonfires all over the islands."

"Could your security men investigate it?" Nan asked hopefully.

Pete looked at the twins and tapped the end of a yellow pencil against his chin as if trying to come to a conclusion.

Finally he said, "You have been right so many times that I don't like to say no."

"Then don't!" Bert grinned.

This made Pete chuckle. "You're both very convincing. But I really can't do it."

"Why not?"

"Listen, Bert. We're going to have record crowds in the next few days, so I'll need all my men. Besides, I really have no right to investigate outside of the World of Fun."

The Bobbseys looked glum and sat silently.

"Oh, cheer up," the security chief said. "You can still be detectives. Maybe your mother or dad can help you scout those islands. You could drive up the coast and rent a motorboat."

Nan's face brightened. "And have our own beach party!" she added.

"There you go," Pete said. "Mix business and pleasure. Not a bad idea. Well, good luck, and let me know what you find out."

"What if we discover a good clue?" Bert asked as they rose to leave.

"Then the state police would step in," Pete replied. "By the way, how long will you be staying in Florida?"

"We're leaving on Wednesday," Nan said. "But we'll be here for the crooks' big job. Will Cherry's plane be ready for them?"

"I'm afraid so," Pete replied. "We can't take

chances with Howie's life." In a low voice he added, "FBI men are all over the place, but you don't recognize them."

The Bobbseys left, disappointed that Pete had regarded their theory so lightly.

"But Mother and Dad will help us," Nan said confidently. "You'll see!"

They trotted along through the morning crowds and soon arrived at the African Village. They stopped short in surprise to see their father walking into the motel office with a suitcase in one hand.

"Hey, Dad!" Bert called out. "Where are you going?"

"Home!" Mr. Bobbsey's forehead was creased with frown lines.

Bert's face fell. "What happened?"

"There was a fire in the lumberyard. I'm catching the next plane to Lakeport."

"Must we go, too?" Nan asked anxiously.

"Well, first I thought all of us should return, but Mother didn't want to spoil your vacation, so she's decided that you children and she will stay."

"Oh, good," Bert said, relieved. "We wanted you to help us scout the islands. Do you think Mother would take us?"

"I'm sure she will," Mr. Bobbsey said. "You know that your mother likes adventures."

Mr. Bobbsey hugged his son and kissed his daughter good-by. "See you at the airport Wednesday." Then he went into the office to tell Mrs. Mingo of his plans.

Walking away, Bert said, "That fire bothers me. I think I smell a rat."

"You mean it was set by our enemies?" Nan asked. "I thought of that, too. But it's kind of far out. Do you really believe the thieves would do that?"

"Why not? They want to get us out of here before the big job!"

"In that case," Nan said, "they got fooled. Only Dad's leaving."

In their parents' hut, Bert and Nan found their mother talking calmly to Freddie and Flossie.

"Don't be upset," she said. "Daddy's lumber-yard didn't burn down *completely*, and nobody got hurt."

"Can we still get wood to build things with?" Freddie asked.

Mr. Bobbsey often brought home short pieces and scraps with which the boys made boats, wagons, and toys. Flossie had a cute doll house that Nan had helped her put together.

Bert said, "We have a lot more detective work to do before we go home." He told of their idea to explore the islands.

"We can do it without Daddy, can't we?" Nan asked.

"Of course."

"When are we leaving?" Flossie bubbled. "I want a 'venture."

"Right now!" Freddie suggested. He always wanted to do things "right now." Mrs. Bobbsey agreed, and the young twins clapped their hands while their mother picked up the phone to order a rental car.

Because a very hot day had been predicted, the twins wore shorts. Mrs. Bobbsey put on a sleeveless blouse and white slacks, and all of them had hats to ward off the brilliant sun.

An hour later the family was driving north along the coast. Bert and Nan, studying a road map, shared the front seat, while Freddie and Flossie sat in the back. They played a game of counting license plates from different states.

"Look, here's a place where we might rent a boat," Bert said. His fingers rested on a town named Tropical Springs. It was located on a small bay not far from a cluster of islands.

"All right," his mother said. "How far is it?"

"About twenty miles."

They all rode along quietly until suddenly Flossie shrieked, "Hawaii!"

Mrs. Bobbsey gave a startled twitch. "Goodness, don't scare me to pieces!" she said, as the car with the Hawaiian license plate drove past.

"I've never seen a Hawaii one before," Flossie said. "I didn't mean to scare you, Mommy."

Freddie said, "I'm hungry."

"We'll have lunch at Tropical Springs," his mother said.

"That's good. How far is it?"

"Fifteen miles."

Freddie kept asking the distance every few minutes until a road sign finally announced that they were there.

"I see a McDonald's," Bert said.

Mrs. Bobbsey stopped and they enjoyed thick, creamy milk shakes and hamburgers. Then they drove down along the bay and parked at a marina full of yachts, cruisers, and motorboats.

A man in khaki shirt and trousers tilted back in a chair outside a shack marked "Office." He rose as they approached.

"Taking your family for a spin?" he asked with a smile.

"Yes. It's a nice day for it," Mrs. Bobbsey replied. "We want a comfortable motorboat, not too fast, not too slow."

"I have the very one you're looking for. Come this way."

The Bobbseys followed the manager to the end of a long catwalk pier, where a sleek blue outboard motorboat rocked lazily in the water.

"She's a beauty," the man said. "Do you know how to handle a motorboat?"

"Oh, yes," Bert replied. "We drive one on our lake at home."

"Good. Here are the keys." He gave them to Bert, and to Mrs. Bobbsey he said, "May I have your name and address?"

As she jotted down the information and paid the required deposit, he quoted the rental rate and wished them good cruising.

"You'll find a small anchor under the seat if you should need it," he said and added, "Oh, yes, there's one thing I must warn you about. Several of these islands are surrounded by sand bars. Be careful you don't get hung up on one, especially when the tide's going out."

"What if we want to land on an island and look around?" Nan said.

The manager said that there were a few narrow channels leading to shore. "But you'd have to know exactly where they are," he said. "A small rowboat could make it, but not this baby."

Bert and Nan helped their mother, Freddie, and Flossie into the boat, then jumped in themselves, sitting down on either side of the tiller.

Nan looked up at the manager as he untied the line and tossed it aboard.

"Did you see the fireworks on the islands last night?" she asked.

"Yes. Quite a show. It beats me how kids can spend so much money and see it go up in the air—*poof!*"

"You think young people did it?" Mrs. Bobbsey asked.

"Nobody lives out there. Only a few shacks the kids built out of driftwood. Be careful, now."

He put his foot against the bow and pushed the boat out, while Bert started the motor. With a gurgling sound the craft backed away. Then they set off toward the islands.

Flossie and Freddie climbed into the bow and looked down to watch the prow cut neatly through the small waves.

"If it gets shallow," Nan called to them, "be sure to tell us!"

Finally the clutch of islands came close enough to be seen clearly. They were no more than barren blisters of sand rising out of the shimmering sea. A few isolated palm trees bent in the breeze near crude little lean-to's made by picnickers.

"People must come out here in rowboats," Mrs. Bobbsey said. "Watch for those sand bars. We don't want to get stuck!"

Taking turns at the tiller, Bert and Nan sur-

veyed the islets, looking carefully for any clue
to the fireworks. Not a thing!

"I just saw a crab!" Freddie exclaimed, trailing his hands in the water.

"Me, too," said Flossie.

"Hey, Bert, I want that stick over there,"
Freddie said.

Bert shielded his eyes from the hot sun and
saw a narrow stick bobbing in the water to the
left of their boat. Nan steered toward it. Freddie
reached out and clutched the prize.

"This is keen," he said. "It's got a thing on
the end."

His mother looked and exclaimed, "It's a
skyrocket! A spent skyrocket! We've found a
clue!"

"Then this must be the island," Nan said.
"This is where the fireworks took place. Come
on, let's try to get ashore."

Bert idled the motor to a purr and headed in
carefully, while Nan climbed into the front to
watch for sand bars.

"Okay. It looks all right," she said as they
came closer and closer.

All at once her attention was drawn to a flash
of light from between two palm trees. "Did you
see that?" she asked.

"See what?" Bert inquired.

"A flash. There it is again!"

"Maybe," Mrs. Bobbsey said, "it's the sun glinting off a bottle."

Then—*thud!*

Everyone pitched forward.

"Good night!" Bert exclaimed. "We've hit a sand bar!"

"We're right on top of it," Mrs. Bobbsey stated, looking over the side. "Oh, dear, and the tide's going out!"

Bert and Nan jumped out and swam beside the boat, hoping to lighten it. Standing on tiptoes they could touch the bottom. They pushed and tugged, to no avail.

"Perhaps I can help," their mother said. She kicked off her sandals and jumped over the side, while Freddie and Flossie watched her with admiration.

More splashing and pushing. But it did not work. They were stuck solidly!

All three climbed over the gunwales and flopped into the boat, dripping wet.

They looked about, hoping to spot another craft that might help, but nothing was in sight!

"They'll search for us sooner or later," Mrs. Bobbsey said with a sigh. She gazed toward the island and gave a startled cry. "I see it too, Nan. That point of light! It's moving!"

Five pairs of eyes trained on the area between the palm trees. Something definitely was moving!

"We've hit a sand bar!" Bert exclaimed.

Then the children let out frightened cries. One—two—three men seemed to rise up from the sand. One had field glasses and looked straight at the Bobbseys!

The wind was blowing from the island toward the Bobbseys' boat, and the men's voices carried plainly over the water.

"It's them, all right!" one said. "They didn't go home, after all. That fire didn't work!"

"Mr. Bobbsey isn't with them," said another. "At least he's gone. And we've got the rest of the family trapped—they can't do anything about it!"

Coarse laughter followed, sending chills through the twins. They were at the mercy of the thieves with no one to help them!

"Spinner, get the flat-bottomed rowboat," the third man commanded, "and bring the prisoners ashore!"

CHAPTER XVIII

HAPPY HOWIE

THE Bobbseys looked on helplessly while two of the three men pulled a rowboat from beneath a pile of driftwood and launched it into the shallow water. One of them manned the oars and started for the stranded family. The third man walked back and vanished between the palm trees.

Flossie started to cry. "They'll hurt us," she sniffled. "What'll we do?"

"I'll fight 'em!" Bert declared, and Freddie said, "Me, too!"

"We'll do nothing foolish," their mother spoke up. "They are probably armed, so please stay calm."

The rowboat came closer, and for the first time the Bobbseys had a good look at the criminals. The rower was thin, and his arm muscles moved like little snakes under his skin. When he glanced over his shoulder, Nan saw him blink his eyes rapidly.

"That one must be Blinky," she whispered to Bert.

Just then Blinky called out, "Hey, Spinner. Did you bring the ropes?"

"Sure. They're in my pocket. Quit the gab and hurry before someone comes along and sees us."

Spinner showed an evil smile at the Bobbseys as the rowboat came alongside. He was taller than Blinky, but just as wiry, and his hairy arms were covered with blue and red tattoos.

In a low tone Bert said, "He must be the man who stole the glass birds and put them in our shopping bag!"

"Easy, now," Spinner said. "We're not going to hurt you. Just do as I say." He stepped into the motorboat, holding short lengths of clothesline in one hand.

"I'm going to tie your hands in back," Spinner said. "Let's begin with the lady. Stand up!"

Mrs. Bobbsey did not budge. "You're being very foolish," she said. "The marina manager knows where we went. He'll come looking for his boat in a little while."

"Stand up, I said!"

"Not until you tell me what this is all about."

The conversation gave Bert and Nan time to look more closely at the two men. Neither appeared to have a gun.

"Don't make me mad," Spinner said. "Get up off that seat!"

Mrs. Bobbsey looked past Spinner and her eyes leveled with those of Bert and Nan. She gave them a slow, sly wink.

"Oh, oh," Nan thought. "Mother's up to something."

Blinky, meanwhile, blinked his eyes faster than ever. "Come on, you're wasting time," he called to Spinner. "Grab her and tie her hands!"

Blinky's scolding and Mrs. Bobbsey's stubborn refusal to move enraged Spinner. He stepped quickly toward her. As he did, she leaned back, pulled her knees up high, and kicked hard with her feet.

"*Oooof!*"

Mrs. Bobbsey's heels caught Spinner in the mid-section, knocking the wind out of him. He reeled backward and landed with a crash at the feet of Bert and Nan, hitting his head on the side of the boat.

Bert pounced upon the stunned man, took the rope from his hands, and quickly tied him up.

Blinky was dumbfounded for a second, then

he quickly climbed out of the rowboat to come to Spinner's help.

But Nan was ready. She grabbed one of his legs and tripped him! When Blinky fell, Freddie and Flossie jumped up and down on top of the surprised thief.

He pushed them roughly aside, and as he tried to get up, Bert hit him on the head with the anchor.

Pow! Down he went again, and Mrs. Bobbsey tied him up without any trouble.

Blinky blinked in amazement at what was happening. "You—you can't do this to us!" he whined. "Wait until the boss comes to pick us up——!"

"You won't be here to tell on us," Freddie chirped, " 'cause we arrested you!"

"Yeah? But you forgot something. You can't get away. Your boat is stuck. And besides, Horsey'll see what happened and come to our rescue!"

"Horsey? Where's he?"

"On the island."

They realized that Horsey must have been the third man!

"Who else is with him?" Nan demanded. "Does he have Howie?"

Blinky started blinking again and set his jaw tightly. He said not a word, but lay there, scowling.

"Mother, let Nan and me go ashore," Bert said. "Since Horsey is probably alone, we might be able to get him, too!"

Spinner, who had now regained his breath, snarled. "Go ahead. Get him. By that time the chief'll be here."

"I think he's bluffing," Mrs. Bobbsey said. "Go ahead, Bert and Nan. If any harm comes to you, those two will answer to me for it!"

The older twins jumped into the rowboat and started for shore. On the way they noticed a cruiser in the distance.

"Oh, dear," Nan said, "maybe that's their boss!"

They stopped rowing for a few minutes and watched anxiously, finally relieved to see the speedy craft disappear on the horizon.

"Wow!" Bert said softly. "We've been lucky so far!"

In a few minutes the bow of the boat hissed onto the white sandy beach. The children hopped out and Bert pulled the boat higher on the shore.

Then they looked around cautiously and listened. Nobody was in sight and everything was quiet except for the wind sighing through the palm trees.

Not far from where they stood, Nan saw a shallow hole in the sand. Bits and pieces of colored paper and splinters of wood lay scattered about. Bert picked up a shredded red tube and smelled it.

"An exploded firecracker," he said. "Nan, this is probably where everything blew up!"

Their eyes scanned the sandy surroundings like radar.

"Over there," Nan said. "Isn't that where the men came out of the ground? Look, Bert, there's a ladder sticking up."

The Bobbseys crept toward the spot. They saw a deep hole in the sand and a wooden ladder leading down.

"It's their hideout," Nan whispered. "Listen, here comes somebody."

They flattened themselves on the sand behind the ladder. Horsey Raines appeared out of the hole. Dangling from his neck on a leather strap was a pair of binoculars. He was the man who had chased Howie around the pool!

Bert let out a bloodcurdling scream as the twins leaped up. He grabbed hold of the strap and jerked the man to the sand, while Nan got a tight lock about his ankles.

"Stop! You're choking me!" Horsey gasped. Bert loosened the strap. By this time he was firmly astride the prone man, pulling his hands behind his back.

"Tie his wrists, Nan!"

The girl removed the binocular strap and bound Horsey's hands together.

Bert let out a bloodcurdling scream.

"Where's Howie?" she demanded.

"None of your business!"

"Check down below," Bert told his sister. "I'll watch our friend here."

Nan climbed down the ladder carefully and found herself in a small den-like room. The puny flame from a small candle cast a yellow glow over a rickety table and spread its feeble light through the rest of the hideout. It was cool and smelled damp.

"Where's Howie?" Nan thought and looked around, her eyes now accustomed to the dimness. Boxes were stacked along one wall. "Probably the stolen goods," she told herself. Behind the table, cast in a heap upon the sand, were two wrinkled bear suits and a Goldilocks costume. The faces looked up at the girl.

"Nan! What are you doing?" Bert called down. "Did you find him?"

"Not yet!"

Scattered about the floor Nan saw soiled paper plates and scraps of food. But no boy.

Then suddenly a bear's face moved and Nan let out a little cry. She ran forward and pulled away the animal outfits.

There lay Howie Norton! He was almost too weak to move. But he smiled wanly. "Thanks for finding me," he said.

Nan helped him to his feet. "Come on, we'll have to get out of here."

Howie walked shakily but managed to climb up the ladder and out into the sunshine.

"Wh-what happened?" he asked, squinting into the bright light.

"We'll tell you later," Bert said. "First let's get back to the boat."

They pulled Horsey to his feet, walked him across the beach, and pushed him into the rowboat.

"Lie down flat on the bottom!" Bert ordered.

The circus man seemed utterly confused. "Spinner! Blinky!" he muttered. "I thought they had caught you!"

"Not quite," Nan said, and added quickly, "Bert, look out there!"

A speedboat was heading directly toward their stranded craft.

"If it's the leader of the mob, we're sunk!" Bert exclaimed.

"That's not the *Circus Princess*," Howie said. "It doesn't have a cabin."

The twins rowed hard, telling Howie how they had found him. By the time they reached the sand bar, they heard happy voices.

"It's the marina man!" Nan said. "Hi, there! See what we have!"

"Howie!" Mrs. Bobbsey and the younger twins were overjoyed to see the boy.

"And I see you've caught the other rascal. Good!" Mrs. Bobbsey said.

"Quite a haul, I'd say," remarked the boat man. "But tell me, why are these men tied up?"

"They're kidnappers and criminals," Bert declared. "They held Howie here on that island, and they stole plenty of stuff from the World of Fun, including fireworks."

"That was a clue," Nan said. "We found a skyrocket stick floating near here."

"I did," Freddie said proudly and held it up for the man to see.

The three prisoners glowered and grumbled.

Spinner said, "It was all your fault, Horsey!" You *would* smoke a cigarette near those fireworks!"

"I didn't know they'd blow up!" Horsey whined. "Besides, you should have covered them with a tarpaulin!"

Blinky blinked nervously. "Shut up!" he yelled. "We're in enough trouble. Don't tell everything!"

"We'll take them to the police," the marina man said. He turned to Bert. "Here, grab a line and tie on the rowboat. Everybody get into my boat and I'll pull you off the sand bar."

"We're awfully glad you came out," Nan said.

"I was worried about you, out here in unfamiliar waters. I figured I shouldn't have let you take the boat in the first place."

"Good thing you did!" Nan said.

Bert made the line secure and gradually their boat was pulled off the bar. It was with a great feeling of relief that Howie and his rescuers made their way back to the marina.

That evening, when he learned what had happened, Pete Prescott was the most surprised man in the World of Fun. And Cherry wept with joy to see her brother safe and sound.

"I wonder if the rest of the gang is going to pull off the big job now," Bert said.

Pete looked thoughtful. "It probably depends on whether they go back to the island and find out what happened. In any case, if the job's still on, we're ready for them, and so is the *Flying Clown.*"

All next day the Bobbseys fidgeted, waiting for something to happen. Had the boss of the gang learned that the island was deserted and fled? Did he have extra men to accomplish the final job?

They played with Howie at their motel, making certain he was not seen outdoors, in case they were being spied upon.

Cherry took up passengers in her plane as usual, but on her last trip of the afternoon not all of them got off. Two FBI men hid themselves in the back of the craft behind the last seats.

The Bobbseys and Howie had pleaded with Pete to let them come to the dock and watch. At first he said no, because it might be dangerous, but finally he gave in.

He took them in a chuck wagon and parked behind some trees in a secluded spot near the seaplane dock. "There are more police hidden all over the place," he said. "But it may be a long wait. Be patient."

An hour went by. Freddie asked for an ice cream cone.

"Not now," Pete said. "I have to stand by the radio, and I don't want any of you to get out."

"Gee, are we going to wait all night?" Flossie asked, as darkness began to fall.

"We might. Especially since we're not sure they're going to pull off a robbery," Pete said.

Then suddenly a chilling message came over the police radio. "London Bridge is falling down!"

"Where did they strike?" Pete asked.

"The bank. Broke into it and got away with the entire payroll. Four masked and armed men. They commandeered a chuck wagon."

"Where are they headed?"

"For the *Flying Clown*."

"Good. Everything's going according to plan."

A few minutes later the headlights of a wagon loomed on the path leading to the dock. The bandits stopped and got out. Carrying sacks of money, they hurried to the plane.

Seconds passed. Then there were shouts and commands and the masked men came out again with hands above their heads.

Pete radioed instructions to his men in the area, who converged on the prisoners and handcuffed them. As Pete and the children ran up, the masks were pulled off the men's faces and they were searched for identification.

Nan cried out, "One of them looks like Horsey Raines!"

"Horsey Raines?" Bert said. "It can't be. He's locked up."

"This is Sam Raines," Pete said. "Here's his driver's license. He's from Chicago. And he has a pilot's license, too."

The prisoner seemed stunned. "My brother's been caught? Impossible! This is all a big bluff. Horsey's holding Howie Morton as a hostage and if you don't let us fly to Mexico, it's all over for the kid!"

His voice was familiar to the Bobbseys. He was the boss!

Howie, who stood behind Bert, stepped up and said, "Really? Well, here I am. The Bobbseys found me and they captured Horsey, Blinky, and Spinner!"

The bandit was tongue-tied with disbelief, and Pete said, "You see? You might as well confess everything."

"Spinner—Blinky—Horsey!" the man muttered. "No wonder I couldn't raise them on the radio this morning!"

The prisoners were led off to be questioned further. After being advised of their constitutional rights, they confessed to all the robberies at the World of Fun, and to having a confederate set fire to Mr. Bobbsey's lumberyard.

They also had bribed a park employee to let them ride up the elevator and hide some loot in the waterfall trough. The "rotten apple" Freddie had suggested really had been a good guess!

Later they had copied the bear outfits, but made a mistake in the number of buttons.

"Good thing they did," Nan said. "That gave them away!"

"The Bobbseys are a pain," Sam Raines said. "They broke a good racket. And that Norton kid is no better. Snooping around all the time!"

The newspapers, as well as television and radio, carried stories about the capture, and the children were praised. On Tuesday, before a huge crowd in front of the Magic Mountain, the Bobbseys and the Nortons were presented with the keys to the World of Fun.

The audience clapped and cheered. Flossie held Howie's hand and said, "Now you don't have to be one of the Old Woman's children any more!"

"I'm happy about that," Howie said. "It was kind of crowded in that bed!"

Freddie spoke up. "There's something else we have to do before we go home."

"What's that?" Pete asked.

"Ride the Rapids. That's one thing we missed."

"Okay, let's go!" Pete said. "You have the keys to everything!"